TRIPPING NITRO

Charon MC
Book 6

KHLOE WREN

Books by Khloe Wren

Charon MC:
Inking Eagle
Fighting Mac
Chasing Taz
Claiming Tiny
Chasing Scout
Tripping Nitro

Fire and Snow:
Guardian's Heart
Noble Guardian
Guardian's Shadow
Fierce Guardian
Necessary Alpha
Protective Instincts

Dragon Warriors:
Enchanting Eilagh
Binding Becky
Claiming Carina
Seducing Skye
Believing Binda

Jaguar Secrets:
Jaguar Secrets
FireStarter

Other Titles:
Fireworks
Tigers Are Forever
Bad Alpha Anthology
Scarred Perfection
Scandals: Zeck
Mirror Image Seduction
Deception

ISBN: 978-0-6483085-2-2

Cover Credits:
Model: Chuck Reid
Photographer: Golden Czermak of FuriousFotog
Digital Artist: Khloe Wren
Editing Credits:
Editor: Carolyn Depew of Write Right

Acknowledgements

Another book done mostly in the last minute because I set myself an insane deadline!

Massive thank you as always to my wonderful husband and girls who continue to put up with all the crazy things I do in order to get my books written in time.

I couldn't have written this book without several people who patiently answered all my many questions about military life and the kink world. Eden, Dawn, Andrea, Stacey (and I'm quite certain there were more and I'm sorry if I missed you by name). Also, a shout out to Sidney Bristol for your derby help and Rachel Rivers for your police and fire protocol help. I can't thank you all enough for your help.

To my editor, Carolyn, no matter what I throw at you, you always come through with a marvelous edit. And this one was super last minute! I appreciate everything you do and thank you for another job well done.

My fb sprint group, the Night Writers, thank you all for the many, many sprints that got this baby done. To my street team, thank you for the support.

xo

Khloe Wren

Biography

Khloe Wren grew up in the Adelaide Hills before her parents moved the family to country South Australia when she was a teen. A few years later, Khloe moved to Melbourne which was where she got her first taste of big city living.

After a few years living in the big city, she missed the fresh air and space of country living so returned to rural South Australia. Khloe currently lives in the Murraylands with her incredibly patient husband, two strong willed young daughters, an energetic dog and two curious cats.

As a child Khloe often had temporary tattoos all over her arms. When she got her first job at 19, she was at the local tattooist in the blink of an eye to get her first real tattoo. Khloe now has four, two taking up much of her back.

While Khloe doesn't ride a bike herself, she loves riding pillion behind her husband on the rare occasion they get to go out without their daughters.

Dedication

To Eden Bradley,
thank you for everything you do and all that you are.

Charon:

Char·on \ˈsher-ən, ˈker-ən, -än\

In Greek mythology, the Charon is the ferryman who takes the dead across either the river Styx or Acheron, depending on whether the soul's destination is the Elysian Fields or Hades.

Chapter 1

Austin, Texas
Nitro

After taking a deep drink of my ice cold beer, I turned to my club brothers with a grin.

"Damn, that's a nice brew."

I was drinking a smooth pale ale from a local microbrewery here in Austin, and it tasted good enough that it had me instantly thinking about how I could get the stuff into Styxx, the bar I ran for my club, the Charon MC, back in Bridgewater.

"Sure is. Tell me, boys, is there anything better than a nice cold beer after a long day's ride?"

In his late fifties, Bulldog was the oldest of the brothers who had come on this run, and the club's VP. Tiny was the youngest at twenty-nine, while Bank and I were in our thirties. I'm sure we made an odd looking group with such a broad range of ages, but we were all wearing our club colors and looked rough as hell after spending the last four days on the road, so I guess we didn't look all that different really. I scratched at the scruff growing over my jaw as I focused for a moment on Tiny's full beard, wondering if I should grow mine out further.

For most of my life I'd kept my face clean shaven, but these last few months I'd found myself letting my scruff grow out more often than not. It wasn't like I had an old lady at home who cared one way or the other, and the club whores didn't give a shit what a brother looked like. The sweet face of the only woman I'd ever truly wanted for an old lady flashed through my mind. It left me wincing and rushing to reach for my beer so I could take a large gulp. Refocusing on my brew, I pushed the memories of her back into the vault where I kept them locked down. I wasn't that love sick, foolish teenager anymore and I hadn't seen or heard from her since the day she vanished from my life all those years ago.

"Well, I'd say a warm bed with my old lady in it would be better, but since that ain't happening this evening, a cold brew ain't a bad way to end a day of riding."

Tiny's comment gave me the distraction I needed to push past the melancholy thinking about her had caused and I laughed easily with the others at his remarks. He and his old lady, Mercedes, only hooked up about five months ago, so were still in the fuck-like-bunnies stage of things. Kinda envied the man that. Mercedes was a good woman.

"Give me a nice cold drink any day of the week, brother."

I hid my grimace behind my glass as I took another mouthful. That was Bank for you, bringing the mood down several notches with one line. The whole club knew his and his woman's relationship was a train wreck waiting to happen. I swore those two spent more time fighting than lovin', so it didn't really surprise me he'd prefer liquor to her. Still, none of us ever knew what the fuck to say to him when he dropped comments like he'd just made, so as per usual, I changed the damn subject and hoped he didn't bring it back up.

Lifting my glass, I looked to Bulldog. "What do you think about getting this one in at Styxx?"

Bulldog gave me a serious nod. "I think it would be a good move. Maybe bring in a few different craft beers from around the area. Microbreweries seem to be all the fucking rage at the moment. Might as well cash in on it, if we can."

"My thoughts exactly, and I've been thinking on this shit for a while now. Actually, I've been thinking about a few different things we could try. Like adding a beer garden to Styxx. Have somewhere outside where folks can sit and relax with a drink."

Bulldog's jaw clenched a moment, which I knew meant he was giving the idea some serious thought, before he gave me another nod. "Yeah, I like the sound of that. Cost that shit out and bring it to church so we can get it moving. The parking lot out back is bigger than we need, so we have the space."

Loud laughter had me turning in my seat to see a group of women who'd just entered the bar. Everything within me froze as my gaze caught on one of them in particular, dressed like a retro pin-up. She wore a high-waisted, skin-tight red skirt that went just below her knees with a slit that went about halfway up the middle of the front, giving me a glimpse of her stocking clad thighs with every step she took. Her top was an equally tight, black button-up shirt that showed plenty of cleavage. It also revealed arms that were heavily inked. Quite simply, she was the hottest woman I'd ever seen. And she seemed vaguely familiar, but I couldn't think where I would have met her before.

Trying to place where I knew her from, I kept my gaze on her as she moved with her group up to the bar, and closer to where we sat in a back booth in the shadows. The low lights over the bar were brighter than elsewhere in the place and when they shone on her, it reflected on the glossy sheen of her chestnut brown hair, making it stand out almost as much as the ink on her arms. Her face swung my way and the breath caught in my throat as I knew exactly who she was.

"Fuck it all."

It must have been nearly twenty years now, since I'd last laid eyes on Cindy, but those blue-gray eyes, those high cheekbones and that sexy as fuck mouth of hers were ingrained in my memory. I scrubbed a hand over my face, trying to get my brain to fucking function properly. Could it really be her? Surely it was just my imagination playing with me because I'd been thinking about her earlier.

"Well, now, those ladies look like a whole lot of trouble."

Bulldog's words had me looking back over at her. She'd always been trouble. In the best possible way. I doubted that had changed.

"That brunette in the blue shirt looks like the bird off that old 'We can do it' poster, don't you think?"

"I'm guessing that was the look she was aiming for. Wonder why they're all dressed up like they are."

At Bank's and Bulldog's comments, I forced my focus from the woman who'd once been the center of my entire fucking universe, taking in the group she was with. There were about a dozen ladies with her and a couple men. A few of the other girls were dressed like her in retro shit, a couple in goth-punk looking outfits, a few others in hippy shit and then a handful of chicks, and the men, that were dressed in normal shit like jeans and shirts. One of the girls was indeed dressed just like a 1940s mechanic, in a pair of short-sleeve, fitted blue overalls. Her dark hair was up with a red bandana wrapped around it.

They were an interesting mix, that's for sure. I frowned when one of the women draped her arm casually over Cindy's shoulders. They were a very affectionate group, too. There was a lot of touching going on between them. Nothing overly sexual, thank fuck, but it was more than I'd ever seen within a group of women. Cindy had needed a lot of hands-on affection as a teen, but that had always been my fucking job. Not her friends'.

"Did you just growl?"

Fuck. Had I?

"Just clearing my throat, brother."

Tiny chuckled before slapping my shoulder. "Brother, you can take as many of them as you like. You don't need to get all growly about it when you're the only single man standing, buddy."

"It ain't like that. The chick in the red skirt? I think that's a girl I knew back in school. She was mine, then one day she was fucking gone. I haven't seen her since."

That was greeted by silence. *Great.* Why the fuck did I just admit all that to my brothers? They'd tell the others and I'd be hearing about it for fucking months. Nothing spread quite like a rumor in an MC did. Especially if the old ladies got wind of it.

Bulldog cleared his throat. "She the reason you came to us in the first place?"

"Yeah."

I didn't need to say more. Bulldog had been there when I'd first started hanging around the club. I'd been nothing but an eighteen-year-old kid, full of rage and aggression. It had been Bulldog, Scout and a few of the others who, after finding out I was about to fuck up my chances at getting into the SEALs, pulled me aside and got me thinking more clearly. They'd helped me train and get ready, and despite the fact the recruiter had me pegged to fail BUD/S, I passed with flying colors. The club had also forced me to come clean with what had happened to fuck me up before they'd agree to help me. So Bulldog knew precisely who Cindy was to me.

"Looks like she's heading back to the bathrooms. Why don't you go have a chat with her where there's some privacy? Clear the air, if nothing else. We've got your back."

After giving my brothers a quick nod, I drained the rest of my beer and after knocking my knuckles on the table, I got up and headed after her. By the time I got to the hallway outside the ladies' bathroom, my palms were sweaty and my heart was beating a mile a minute. What the fuck should I say? Was it really her? Would she remember me?

Before I could plan out anything, she pushed through the door and my world narrowed down to just her. Taking her in, I wiped my palms on my jeans, and tried to prepare for her reaction to seeing me. Because now I was this close, I knew it was her. She hadn't changed that much over the years. Sure, she'd filled out some, gotten curvier, sexier. But her face, her hair, that was the same. And I was dying to touch her again.

"Hey, Cin. It's been a long time, huh, babe?"

Cindy

With my head down, it wasn't until I heard a throat clearing that I realized I wasn't alone in the hallway.

Then he'd spoken. That voice. That rough, familiar voice of his shot straight down my spine, just like it always had. The shock of hearing it again after so long had me stumbling, but he didn't let me fall. Nope, Jonathan Harris had never once let me fall. Even when I'd begged him to let me go, he'd refused, forcing me to make the choice to leave my home and Bridgewater when I'd been seventeen to keep us both safe.

I couldn't hold in the gasp that slipped free when his warm, callused palms wrapped around my bare biceps, keeping me on my feet. My eyes slid shut as memories of our time together bombarded my senses. I'd had a crush on Johnny since my first week as a freshman, but it wasn't until I'd been a sophomore that he'd finally noticed me. But the wait had been worth it. He'd been such an attentive and patient boyfriend. From the moment we connected, he only had eyes for me and was always so sweet and protective. We'd dated for nearly a full year before we took it further and I gave him my virginity.

We'd had it all.

Then we didn't.

The beginning of the end was the day after my parents were seriously injured in a car crash, when I'd received the first threat. I'd found it in our mailbox after I'd returned from visiting my parents in the hospital. A rough, hand-written note, claiming responsibility for the accident and telling me worse would happen if I didn't cut all ties with Johnny.

I'd only been sixteen fucking years old, and suddenly forced to deal with shit a teenage girl shouldn't have to. Mom had only suffered a broken arm and a concussion from the wreck, but Dad had nearly died from his various injuries. He'd ended up having to stay in the hospital for weeks. From the get-go, Mom had been preoccupied with recovering herself and caring for Dad. That resulted in her not taking the letter I'd received seriously. She'd told me the crash had been an accident. When Dad swerved to miss a feral pig that had run out in front of them, their car had left the road and ended up running into a tree. Not really seeing how someone could have created the accident, I believed Mom and followed her advice to simply ignore it. That, and I didn't want to break up with Johnny. He was always so damn sweet with me, making sure I'd eaten and had a ride to school each day. The last thing I'd wanted to do was push him away. I wanted him as close as I could get him.

I'd found the second letter in my locker at school a few days later. That one had made it very clear that whoever was writing them was really angry with me. Apparently, since I'd not been listening and being a *bad girl*, I'd needed to be taught a lesson. I'd gotten home from school that afternoon to find my sweet cat, Whiskers, dead on the front lawn. He'd been hit by a car and just left there for me to find.

Even then, Mom still didn't take the threats seriously, and neither did the police. When I'd taken the letters in, they'd told me it was nothing but some kid in my class claiming the accidents for their own to upset me. Cats got run over all the time, apparently. But I'd been so damn scared of what this nut-job would do next, I'd done the only thing I could at the time. I gave in. I'd broken up with Johnny—well, I'd tried to. He'd assumed I'd been just overwhelmed with everything and not thinking clearly, so he'd told me he'd back off but he wasn't going anywhere. So I'd then done what teenagers do best when they found themselves backed into a corner. I ran.

"Ah, fuck. Cin, are you okay? I didn't mean to scare you."

I melted a little more at him calling me Cin. Everyone else called me Cindy. One of his palms stayed on my bicep, while the other slid up until it was wrapped around the back of my neck, then his thumb began to stroke the side of my throat. Just like he used to do back in school right before he'd kiss me.

Reality came crashing down. I couldn't afford to get close to Johnny, my stalker would find out and make me pay. Or him. Twisting out of his grip, I quickly glanced up and down the hallway, searching for people in the darkness who might be watching us. There were two men at the end of the hallway with their backs turned to us but that didn't mean they weren't watching. I had no idea who my stalker was, even all these years later, so I had no idea who to watch out for. Before I could make my getaway, Johnny's hand shackled my wrist.

"Let me go, Johnny. I need to get out of here."

"Whoa. Stop right there. Why are you so fucking scared? It can't be me. I'd never hurt you, you know that. Is someone threatening you? Tell me who and I'll deal with the fucker."

Tears pricked my eyes at his words. *Always so fucking protective.* It would be easy to cave in to him, but then what? The last time I'd dared to test if my stalker was still watching, I'd gone out to dinner with a man. I woke the next morning to discover my car had been keyed down the entire length of both sides, and I'd received another note. I'd reported the damage to the police, who still didn't take it seriously. Whoever it was hadn't done anything to harm me, and my car apparently could have been damaged by accident. Just like back in school when both Mom and the police wrote it all off without a second thought. I hadn't even bothered to tell them about the note.

Although, I think the reason the police brushed it off then was because of my involvement with Her Royal Hellions, the roller derby team I was a member of. We had a bit of a reputation for being wild and rough, which apparently meant we didn't get to be included under the protection of the men in blue. So after that incident, I'd decided I wouldn't bother telling anyone at all about anything else my stalker did. Clearly, no one was ever going to believe me, so why bother. I also decided it was simply easier, and safer, to stay single. Even if I did get so fucking lonely being on my own all the time.

Blinking away the moisture gathering in my eyes, I kept scanning the hallway.

"I-" Fuck, I wanted to lie. To tell him I barely remembered him, that he should go away and leave me alone, but my tongue refused to form the words. Maybe it was the hard glint in his eyes, so much like the Doms I saw at the BDSM club, Titanium, where I tended the bar, that had me trembling as my heart fought against my mind on what the hell I should do.

"This is fucking bullshit, Cindy."

Releasing my wrist, he shifted to cup my face as he'd done earlier, then tilted it up toward his. Emotion clogged my throat. No one had ever held me like he had, and still did.

"Johnny…"

His gaze was fixed on my lips and I knew what he was about to do. I knew I should stop him. Kick him in the shins or something, then run like hell. It was the only way to save us both. But that's not what I did. Not what I really wanted. For the past eighteen years, eight months, two weeks and three days, my heart, soul, body and mind had been craving this man. Not that I'd been counting or anything.

My mind shut down as instinct and desire took over. Pressing my palms against his solid, muscular chest, I leaned into him as his face descended.

His growl filled my ears a moment before his lips brushed over mine. It was a gentle touch, like he was testing his welcome. It wasn't enough. Not nearly enough. I pushed up onto my tiptoes and boldly nipped at his lower lip before pressing my mouth solidly over his. That move earned me another growl, then he stopped screwing around and took control of our kiss. I slipped my tongue out to greet his when he licked at my lips. The kiss held none of the finesse I knew he had. It was hot, passionate, a little messy, and rapidly had me breathless. I pulled away to take a breath and his grip tightened on my face.

"Get back here, Cin. I'm not nearly done with you."

Stroking my palms down his front and around to grip his hips, I smiled up at him and accepted another of his kisses. This one was a little slower, it was Johnny in full-on seduction mode. It had my brain spinning and my heart tripping over itself. Kissing Johnny was everything I remembered and more. This was no longer a boy but a man. A strong, powerful dominant man. I doubted he was a trained Dom like the men at Titanium, but now that I was back in his arms, feeling him against me again. I knew why I'd always felt so comfortable around those men. Without realizing it, I'd gravitated toward them because they'd reminded me of what I'd left behind. Of what I'd craved. Not that I'd ever indulged. I couldn't risk my stalker finding out if I did, so I'd stayed behind the bar and simply observed what the others did before going home and taking care of myself.

That had a sob catching in my throat. I was being stupid. So fucking stupid. I tore myself away from him and swiping the tears from my eyes, I ran down the hallway, out to find my team, wishing I had my skates on. I'd be able to get out of here so much faster if I was on my wheels. I needed to get out of the bar and up to my room before Johnny came after me, which I knew he'd do within seconds of me bolting. The fact we weren't in Houston hopefully meant my stalker wasn't here watching my every move.

My gaze caught Natalie's and with a frown, she excused herself from the others and came straight over to me.

"What on earth happened? Do I need to go deal with someone?"

Another sob escaped, and I raised my hand to cover my mouth. Along with being the captain of Her Royal Hellions, Natalie was the owner of Titanium. She was also a Domme, who took no shit from anyone. Even though I'd turned down her offer to train me as a submissive, that hadn't stopped her from taking me under her wing. She was as protective as Johnny, and one of my closest friends.

"I'll explain later, but right now, I need to get out of here."

"Damn straight you'll explain. C'mon, we'll head up to your room."

Leaning into her when she wrapped her arm around my shoulders, I kept my gaze down and let her lead me out of the bar. My mind was spinning while my lips still tingled from Johnny's kisses. I was so fucking torn about what to do. Part of me wanted to turn around and run back to Johnny, to be wrapped up in his arms as I told him everything and hoped he could somehow magically fix it all. But the bigger part of me, the part that was used to living half a life in order to stay safe, won out like it always did and allowed Natalie to guide me out of the hotel bar and into an elevator.

"Assuming this has something to do with the hot biker who came barreling out of the hallway after you, you sure know how to pick 'em, babe."

After wiping the tears from my cheeks and trying to regain some level of composure I faced her.

"Biker?"

She cocked a brow in surprise. "What the hell happened between the two of you in that hallway that you didn't seem to notice that man was wearing Charon MC colors?"

Feeling like the breath had been knocked out of me, I reached out a hand for the wall to steady myself.

"Oh, fuck."

The Charon MC ruled Bridgewater. That meant he'd stayed local. Bridgewater was only about an hour from Houston. I hadn't ever seen many of the Charons riding around Houston but they did on occasion. Would he find me again? We were in Austin right now, but we were at a hotel so I doubted he'd think I lived here. What would happen when my stalker discovered Johnny was back in my life?

The ding of the elevator arriving at our floor had me pulling out of my thoughts long enough to follow Natalie down the hallway. Pulling my keycard out, I made fast work of opening things up. Once we were inside the room and the door was shut, she didn't waste a moment.

"Come and sit down, sugar. I'll grab us something to drink and then you can explain to me what the fuck just happened downstairs."

Obediently, I went and sat at the table while Natalie grabbed a couple bottles of water. I was rubbing my temples when she set the bottle in front of me before taking a seat in the chair opposite me. Looking into her dark eyes, I opened my mouth but couldn't find the words. My thoughts were all jumbled and messy. Closing my mouth, I pressed my fingers against my lips that still tingled from his kisses. Where did I start? How much did Natalie want to know? How much *should* she know? If I told her everything, would she try to find my stalker to handle him herself? She could get hurt. Or worse, would she not believe me and tell me I was being stupid. I couldn't lose my place on the team, or my job at Titanium.

"Cindy?"

Natalie was using her Domme voice and it had everything in me stilling.

"Yes, ma'am?"

"Take a couple of deep breaths and drink some water." She stopped talking while I followed her instructions. By the time I recapped the bottle I felt much calmer but still wasn't sure where to start. "The time has come for you to tell me your whole story, Cindy. No more hiding. Who is that man to you?"

I shook my head. "He's no one anymore. But he was once my whole world. We dated in high school."

Once I started, it all flowed out of me. I gave Natalie everything. From my and Johnny's first kiss, to me running away after the second threat, to my car getting keyed after I risked going on a date, and how grateful I was to her and Titanium for giving me a safe place I could relax and enjoy myself. Even if I didn't take full advantage of it.

By the time I finished speaking, it felt as though a great weight had been lifted from my shoulders. I'd never told anyone everything in one hit like that before. When I'd first joined Her Royal Hellions and then when I'd started to work at Titanium, I'd given Natalie and the others the barest amount of information about my history as I could get away with. I hadn't wanted them to turn away from me. It was that fear that had me still tense now, despite the lightness I felt from having unloaded it all. The fear Natalie was about to reject me had me on edge.

"So much makes sense now. You should have told me everything a long time ago, but I can understand why you didn't. That's why you refuse to get out from behind the bar at the club, isn't it?"

I nodded. "I couldn't risk my stalker somehow finding out. I have no idea who it is, so I don't know when he's close to me."

"I hope like hell we didn't let that fucker in, but without knowing who he is, there's no way of knowing for sure. Fuck, I'm so sorry you've been living like this for so long. It's not natural, or healthy."

I couldn't hide my shock. "You believe me, then?"

With a frown, she cocked her head to the side. "Why wouldn't I believe you?"

"No one else has. My parents and the police have never believed anything I've told them. Even when I showed them the notes, they always had a way to explain it away."

"Well, I've got no fucking clue why they didn't believe you, but I do, and the team will back you up too, when you're ready to tell them. And the sooner you do, the sooner everyone can keep an eye out and we might just be able to figure out who this bastard is. We take care of our own, and we'll get to the bottom of it. Well, that's if we get the chance. Now the Charons are involved I dare say your life is about to get really interesting, sugar. Those men aren't exactly known for sitting back and letting shit like this slide by, even if it's happening to someone not involved with the club. Given Johnny seems to be re-staking his claim on you? They'll have it all sorted out in no time, I'm sure"

"You think he'll find me again? I mean, we're pretty far from home right now."

She patted my hand as she snorted out a laugh. "Oh, honey, I can guarantee you, that man will find you again. And soon."

Fear and excitement mixed inside me, I couldn't work out if I wanted him to find me again or not. And was Natalie right? Would he and his club really be able to sort out my stalker issue? Assuming they even believed me.

Chapter 2

Nitro

It was late evening by the time we got back to the clubhouse, but I didn't waste time once we arrived before I had Keys, the club's secretary and resident tech guy, looking for info on Cindy. No way was I letting that girl slip through my fingers again. Not with how she fucking kissed me. I had no idea what the fuck was going on with her, or the real reason behind her leaving town when were in school, but I was certain it wasn't because she didn't want me—which is what I'd always thought had been the case.

"C'mon, man. Can't you make all this shit work faster already?"

Keys raised an eyebrow at me as he continued to tap away at his laptop.

"If you want to have a go, I'll happily leave you to it. I'd much rather be out there with my old lady than in here with your grumpy ass."

That had me grimacing. Most of the club was out in the yard around the bonfire, enjoying themselves. I knew

Keys didn't have to be in here putting up with my bullshit.

"Fuck, I'm sorry, brother. It's just, last night, I got this feeling she was being watched or chased or something, I want to fucking know what's going on with her." *So I can fix it and bring her home with me where she belongs.* I didn't say that out loud, but I was fairly certain Keys knew I was thinking it. "How about I get out of your hair for a bit and go grab us a drink?"

Giving him a break from my shit, I left him to it for a few minutes while I went out to the bar to grab us both a drink. The clubhouse was in full night time mode with brothers and club whores all over the place. I should have been over at Styxx, checking that it was all running well, especially since I'd been out of town for the past five days, but when Scout had heard about what had happened with Cindy he'd told me he'd get the bar taken care of until I got shit sorted.

Not wanting to chat, I kept my head down, and managed to get the drinks and get back out of the main room fairly quickly. After I returned, I set Keys' drink in front of him before taking a seat myself. Keys was a fucking genius on a computer and I had no doubt he'd get me the information I needed. I just wished he'd find it faster. Or that I could be more patient. But dammit, I've been waiting, what? Nineteen years for her. I was done waiting. And I had a feeling that whatever it was that had her so damn nervous was going to come for her sooner rather than later. I intended to be there when it did.

"Right, well, what I have so far on your Miss Cindy Davis is… she shares an apartment in Houston with another woman, Renee Stock. She works two part-time jobs, sales assistant at a small store called Retro Funk and bar-tending at a place called Titanium. She's also into roller derby. She's part of a team called Her Royal Hellions. Her roommate is also on the team. You should check out their site. They're actually pretty good by the looks of it and your girl is all over their site in photos and clips." He paused to take a drink, staring at me while he did. "If she means this much to you, why haven't you gone looking for her before now? I mean, from what I've found she moved to Houston after she left Bridgewater at sixteen and stayed there."

I shrugged at his query. "I did all I could to find her when she first left, but I was a fucking kid, man. Didn't know the first thing about how to find someone who didn't want to be found. Her parents had just been in a bad car wreck, her dad was seriously hurt. I forget what his injuries were exactly, but he was in hospital for a long damn time. Her mom didn't get as badly hurt, but she'd still been injured and between recovering herself and trying to help her husband, she was too busy to have time for a lovesick teenage boy looking for their daughter. Especially considering she knew Cin broke up with me before she left. Then, when I came back from the Navy, it had been over ten years. I figured she'd be long gone, settled down somewhere with a husband and two-point-five kids. But that's not the fucking case. That girl was scared of something. Like petrified, and that's got me wondering about what really happened all those years ago. Because it wasn't like we had a fight or anything. One day my world was sunshine and roses, the next it had gone to hell. No warning."

Keys leaned forward, holding my gaze with his own. "I can get you all the facts and figures you want, but I doubt the internet is gonna tell me the answers you need. Why don't you go see her parents now?"

I shook my head before I finished off my drink. "They moved while I was deployed. No fucking clue where they are anymore."

He scribbled something down on a piece of paper. "Well, here's the addresses for Cindy's apartment and the shop where she works. She normally works Tuesdays, so how about a few of the boys and I come with you for a ride up to Houston tomorrow and you can see about getting her to agree to lunch or something. Word's already spread about how she ran out of that fucking bar in Austin. Bulldog thinks like you do about her being scared. So I'd recommend starting off gentle with her, and stick to public settings. Until you know the lay of the land, so to speak."

Scrubbing a palm over the back of my neck, I reached out with my other hand and took the note. "Yeah. I know I need to go slow with her. But it's gonna fucking kill me to be so close to her and not have her."

He started shutting down his laptop. "The right woman will do that to a man, brother. The whole club has your back on this. Whatever it ends up being after her, we'll deal with it."

With a nod I stood and we both headed out to the main room. I headed straight for the bar for another drink, but before I could make it I had one of the club whores in my face looking for some attention. With a shake of my head I moved past her, but I didn't make it far before I had another one in my face telling me she could improve my mood. After dealing with her, I decided that a drink just wasn't worth the trouble, so I turned to head toward the stairs. It was probably a better idea for me to get a good night's sleep before tomorrow, anyhow. Because tomorrow I would find a way to get Cindy to fucking tell me what the hell was biting at her heels that had her looking so fucking scared in Austin.

Cindy

I loved Tuesday mornings at Retro Funk. The shop was always quiet this early, so my aunt would hide away in the back after telling me what I should do. *Like I didn't know after working here for the past nineteen years.* Within the first week of moving in with Grandma, I'd started to come with her into the store to help out. While I'd still been in school, I came in on the afternoons and weekends, then when I finished up high school, I'd decided against heading off to college. I loved this store and Houston. I hadn't wanted to leave and hadn't seen the point. Not when I had a job I loved in a shop I adored.

Retro Funk had been my grandma's pride and joy. She'd carefully selected every piece of stock she had. From the clothes to the trinkets, it was all a reflection of her heart. And mine. Once I moved in and she saw how much I loved all the retro pin-up stuff, she started getting more of it in. Everyone who lived anywhere near the store knew us both on sight, I was always dressed up like a funky 1950s chick, while Grandma had been a hippy. Until the day she died Grandma had worn her flowing skirts and beads in her hair. I rubbed over the ache in my heart that happened whenever I thought of Grandma. We were kindred spirits and I missed her terribly.

She'd always been so accepting of everyone, no matter who they were. Even knowing that, it had still surprised me at first when she didn't bat an eyelash at me suddenly deciding to move in with her. I never could bring myself to tell her about the threats I'd been getting. My parents and even the cops didn't take them seriously, I wouldn't have been able to handle my grandmother saying the same thing. I'm sure she realized something was going on, but she never asked me about it. Nope, she just opened her arms wide and welcomed me home.

I blinked away the tears that pricked my eyes. I missed her so much. She'd been gone for twelve years now, but time didn't lessen the pain of my grief. Losing Grandma had hit me hard, and before I could even really begin to process it, certain family members decided it was best to sell Grandma's house as quickly as possible, leaving me homeless. To top that off, I got informed that her will revealed that, despite the fact I'd worked alongside Grandma six days a week since I'd finished high school and she knew I loved the store, she hadn't left it to me. Mom tried to explain to me that it was because Grandma loved me and wanted me to live my life and follow my dreams, not get stuck living hers. When Mom had seen how upset over it I was, she'd managed to convince my other aunt and uncles that Grandma would have wanted me to have the option to work in the store as long as I wanted to.

Honestly, I didn't fully understand how that side of it all worked, whether my Aunt Skye signed some kind of contract when she took over Retro Funk or what. I'd asked her more than once, but she always refused to answer. Clearly, it meant my aunt couldn't fire me. Unfortunately, it hadn't stopped her from cutting my hours back. At a guess, she wanted me to quit and just leave her to it, but I refused. Even if I only got one and a half days a week, I was going to make the most of it, spending every moment I could in this place that reminded me of Grandma.

I'd been twenty-four years old when all that had happened. I'd been on Her Royal Hellions derby team for a couple years by then and thankfully, they'd already fully accepted me into their little derby family. I was still grateful for that when I'd gone to them feeling completely devastated about the turn my life had just taken. That I'd suddenly found myself with a double dilemma, I'd needed somewhere to live and another job. The girls had jumped to help me out. Renee offered me the spare room in her apartment, where I still lived, and they told me about Titanium for the first time.

Before that day, I'd heard the girls mention the club's name on occasion, but I'd had no clue what type of club it was or what went on there. I'd been so excited to seemingly have all my problems solved at once, I honestly didn't give a damn what type of club it was! Natalie, who had already been our team captain even back then, owned Titanium, and she'd mentioned she needed a reliable bartender at the club. Before she'd take my answer on the job offer, she'd told me I had to come with her for a private tour. I hadn't realized until later that I'd been basically the only Hellion who wasn't a member. I'd also had no clue what BDSM was. Not only had I not had sex since leaving Johnny, but I hadn't had any intimacy at all. I couldn't risk it and my stalker seeing. Not after the damage to my car after that one date when all we did was have a quick kiss at the end of the night. I shuddered to think what he'd do if I tried anything like that again. The note he'd left had been very clear things would escalate if I continued to defy him.

As requested, I'd gone in after hours with Natalie and she'd walked me around the entire club and answered all my questions. She'd told me that as an employee, I would also be a member and I was welcome to play in the club whenever I wasn't working. But there was no pressure—if I wanted to stay behind the bar and never play, that was fine too. It would be completely up to me. I'd told her I was simply happy to have a job, and I'd kept my ass planted firmly behind the bar all these years, even though I often got asked to scene with various Doms. After so many years, I'd heard all sorts of rumors about why I didn't date or scene at all.

Aunt Skye clearing her throat pulled me from my trip down memory lane. Shaking my head, I turned to face her and my mind spun while my blood froze in my veins, forcing me to grip the counter for balance. Because she wasn't alone. Nope, he'd tracked me down. Dammit. Johnny was standing beside Aunt Skye, looking at me with an indulgent look in his gaze, like he'd known my mind had been wandering. My aunt's expression wasn't nearly as nice. She looked peeved off that I'd been lost in thought. *Nothing unusual there.*

"This young man is here to see you, Cindy. Why don't you take your lunch break early?"

Yeah, because heaven forbid I talk on the job. Aunt Skye was nothing like my grandmother, and it made me miss her all the more. Forgetting about my stalker for the moment, and needing to get away from my aunt and her bullshit for a while, I readily agreed and headed out the door with Johnny by my side.

"Well, that was a lot easier than I thought it would be."

"Don't get too excited. You caught me when I really needed a break, and this has to look like we're just friends catching up. So don't try any funny business. I can't risk it."

He chuckled and reached for my hand as if I'd not said a word. With a growl I pulled mine out of his reach. "I'm serious, Johnny. You can't do shit like that, it's dangerous."

He stayed silent as we walked further up the street. Without touching me, he indicated I go ahead of him into a small cafe. Once inside, I followed him as he made his way to an empty table against the back wall. As I moved between the tables, I noticed that there were a few other men wearing the same vest as Johnny, sitting at the tables around the one he chose for us. There seemed to be Charons everywhere in here and it had me nervous. What the fuck was he playing at?

"What the hell is going on, Johnny? What is this?"

What was he planning? Was he going to snatch me and take me away or something? I tried to back away but he reached over and shackled my wrist in his hand and pulled me closer to him.

"No one calls me Johnny anymore, I go by Nitro now. And relax, I'm not trying to pull shit with you here. With how you acted in Austin, I figured you might be in some sort of trouble. That, together with what you said to me when we walked out of your shop confirms my suspicions. I came to find you today to get you to tell me what's going on so I can fix it. My club brothers came with me to make sure you stay safe while that happens, nothing more. I promise."

That had my stomach twisted into tight knots. I didn't want to tell him anything. As much as I hoped he'd be like Natalie and believe me, what if he wasn't? I wasn't sure I could handle seeing a look of rejection in his eyes. I needed to get out of here, away from him before I caved. I'd been lonely for so long now, I knew deep inside it wouldn't take much for him to get under my skin again, to have me telling him, giving him, everything he asked for. I tried to twist my wrist free from his tight grip, but he wouldn't budge. His hand tightened on me, not enough to hurt but enough to make it clear I wasn't going anywhere until he decided to let me go.

"Stop trying to run off, babe. Just sit down with me and we'll have lunch. That's all I'm asking for."

No it wasn't. He was asking for more so much more. He wanted my secrets. *So he can protect you.* My subconscious had always been Team Johnny. Maybe I could give him just a little of the truth and see how he reacted. If he looked like he was going to be like my mom, I'd stop talking and walk out of here. I was sure if I started to cause enough of a scene, he'd let me go. Because if he did follow my Mom's lead, I didn't want him back in my life. But if he was instead like Natalie, it might be nice to have someone like him in my corner for once. Maybe, just maybe, it was time for me to take a risk and attempt to start living my life again.

Chapter 3

Nitro

The flush that rose in her cheeks as she tried to free her hand from my grip had me wanting to grin, but I fought it down, not wanting to frustrate her any more than I already had. But damn, she was still the sexiest woman I'd ever laid eyes on. Fuck, I wanted to strip her out of her pin-up outfit right now and claim her for my own again. Wanted to get my hands and mouth onto her, get my cock deep inside her. Because, fuck it all, but this woman was *mine*. Always had been, always would be.

When she still hadn't made a move to sit down, I shifted my grip onto her hand, lifting it so I could kiss the backs of her fingers. A shudder ran through me as I inhaled her scent, fresh and floral, just like it had been back in school. She must still use the same body wash even all these years later. My cock, which had been hard since the moment I saw her standing in the middle of Retro Funk staring off into space, jerked behind the fly of my jeans, growing even harder and begging for some attention. Unfortunately, since there was no way for me to rearrange things discretely, I was just going to have to put up with the discomfort for the moment. I wasn't sure how Cin would handle knowing how desperate I was for her, but considering how skittish she was, I didn't think it would go over well. Her behavior also made me even more determined to get her to tell me what was going on. Something that became more likely to happen when, with a sigh, she finally gave in and sat down. I followed suit, and sat opposite her at the little table I'd led us to. Not wanting to waste any more time, I asked what I wanted to know.

"Why did you really leave Bridgewater all those years ago? Does it have something to do with what has you running scared now?"

Her eyes welled with moisture, leaving me wincing. Fuck it all, maybe I should have eased into the questions rather than jumping straight in. Ah well, too late now. But I needed to get her to understand she could tell me anything, that I'd handle whatever it was.

"Cin, I'm not an eighteen year old kid anymore, I've spent ten years in the Navy, as a SEAL. I'm a member of the Charon MC. And every one of my club brothers will help me keep you safe, I just need you to lean on me. Let me help you, tell me what's got you scared to live your life."

An extremely brave waitress chose that moment to interrupt us, and after we both ordered the special, which I ordered without having a fucking clue about what it was, she left us to it.

"So many haven't believed it."

Her voice was small, almost a whisper.

"You know me better than that, you know I'll always believe you. Well, except if you tell me you're fine, that I won't believe. Nor will I leave you alone."

She shook her head as she looked up and blinked rapidly. Dammit, I didn't want to make her cry. The waitress brought over two glasses of iced tea before leaving us again.

"I have no idea who it is. Never have."

My heart started to ache. I'd been right, dammit. Someone was fucking with her, and she'd been suffering through it with no fucking help all these years. I pushed down my anger that she'd not trusted me with what was going on back then, because from here on out, she was going to fucking trust me with it.

"What happened that July, when you broke up with me and left town?"

She glanced around us. My gaze followed hers and I knew my brothers at the table closest to us were the only ones who might hear what she said. The others were out of ear shot, not that it mattered. If they did hear, they wouldn't let on. And if they didn't, they'd be hearing the story from me at church.

"After the car accident, I got a note. It had been hand delivered to the mailbox at home. It said they'd caused the accident and that if I didn't cut all ties with you, worse would happen. I told Mom about it and she told me it was a prank, to ignore it." My heart clenched when she paused to use her napkin to dab at her eyes. "The next one was in my locker at school. That was on the day Whiskers died."

I winced as I remembered that day. She'd been so upset when she'd told me she couldn't see me anymore. I'd figured she'd just been overwhelmed with her parents' accident and the loss of her pet, I didn't take her request seriously. I loved her, and wanted to be there for her, not leave her hanging when she was so clearly hurting, so I'd refused to accept her leaving me.

"That's why you left? Because I refused to allow you to break up with me?"

Her body shuddered as she pressed the napkin to both her eyes, hiding her face from me. Her shoulders rose and fell as she took a deep breath, before she lowered the paper and lifted her red-rimmed eyes to mine.

"It sounds fucking stupid when you say it like that, but I was a kid. No one would believe me. Mom said cats got hit all the time by cars, that the notes were just some bully being cruel and screwing with me. The police agreed with her. I did the only thing I could think to do, and that was getting the hell out of town. With Mom being so busy, it wasn't hard to convince her and Dad to let me move up to Houston to live with Grandma."

"And did you get more notes after the move?"

She nodded her head before she reached for her glass of iced tea.

"It was years later before I got brave enough to risk going out on a date. We went out for a nice dinner, but the entire night I was so nervous that my stalker would do something. He ruined the night without having to lift a finger. My date gave me a brief kiss at the end of the night and I never heard from him again. Then, the next morning I discovered my car had been keyed up both sides—I had to park out on the street when I lived with Grandma—and another note was in the mailbox. He was still watching. Well, at least I assume it's a man. I guess it could be a woman. I've honestly got no fucking idea."

The waitress turned up with our food and I used the time to try to get my temper under control. This bastard had been fucking with her for nearly twenty years. She'd had basically no life outside of work thanks to his stalker bullshit.

"He leaves you alone at roller derby games?"

She picked at the fries that came with her burger for a few moments. "I've never received a note from him about it, so I guess he doesn't have a problem with me being close to other women. He doesn't seem to have an issue with me working at Titanium either, although I suspect that's more because he's not found his way inside, but I could be wrong."

Her face flushed again and I didn't think it was anger that had her suddenly very interested in her burger.

"What kind of place is Titanium?"

She just shook her head as she chewed, refusing to answer my question. *Interesting.* Guess I'd have to get that one out of her later.

"Do you really think you'll be able to catch this guy?"

Of course I did. In fact, her lack of faith in me was a little insulting, to be honest, but I didn't get mad at her over it. She didn't know who'd I'd become since high school.

"Hell yeah, I do. One of my brothers, Keys, is really good on a computer. He's going to be setting up some cameras outside of your apartment building and he's hacked access to the feeds on the cameras outside Retro Funk, Titanium and where you train for your derby thing. We're going to keep watch for anyone who shows up at all three places more often than they should. I'm also going to have a couple of the prospects hang around near you at all times—"

She held a palm up to stop me talking as she finished her mouthful.

"Seriously? What the fuck? Not to mention all the laws this friend of yours has just broken, I will not be made to feel like a… a science experiment that is being constantly examined!"

Shocked that she'd see things that way, I tried to gentle my tone. "Cindy, isn't that how this bastard has made you feel for the last what—nineteen years? This will only be for a little while, just until we catch this fucker. I will make sure you stay safe, babe, so you can start living your life again. Whoever this is, has stolen more than enough from us both. I won't let them take any more."

She went from looking hopeful to defeated. "But the cops won't believe us, even if we do catch him doing something."

I couldn't prevent the feral grin that spread over my lips. "Babe, you grew up in Bridgewater. You know what my club is capable of. It won't matter a lick what the police think, justice will be served. I can guarantee you that."

With that, I let the topic drop and began to eat my lunch. Throughout the rest of the meal our conversation stayed light. She told me stories about her derby family and I shared a few stories from both my Navy days and my Charon family. I hoped like hell when all this was over that she'd be moving back to Bridgewater with me. I needed her in my life. She was the missing puzzle piece that had prevented me from truly being content, no matter what I did.

Cindy

After lunch, Johnny, I mean Nitro, had walked me back to the shop before he headed off. He'd wanted to take me out to dinner after I finished work, but I'd refused his offer. I wasn't sure he realized what could potentially happen after our lunch. If my stalker had seen any of it, anything could happen. I had no clue what having Nitro back in my life would do to him, even if we didn't do anything romantic. Nitro was the thing that initially set off this nut-job so it made sense him coming back into my life would send him over the edge again.

Thankfully, I worked a full day at the store on Tuesdays, and the afternoon was busy enough I didn't end up with time to dwell on any of it. But as five o'clock crept closer and the customers dried up, I found myself with way more time to think. To wonder if telling Nitro had been the right thing to do, to over-analyze, and basically get myself totally worked up over every possibility.

"I'm being stupid. This is just like every other Tuesday."

After giving myself a little pep talk as I locked up, I hopped in my car and headed from the shop back to my apartment to get changed for practice. It was strange to have two Harleys follow me the whole way, but at least this time I knew for sure I was being watched. Over the years, the not knowing where or when I was being spied on had just about driven me insane at times.

When I pulled up outside practice, the rumble of the bikes got louder as I got out of my car and they pulled up behind me. Not sure what exactly they were planning to do, I went to talk to them.

"Um, I'm going to be here for hours so you really don't need to hang around."

"Ma'am, if Nitro found out we left you unprotected, our lives would be shortened considerably."

"Yeah, he'd fuck us up like you read about."

I couldn't help but chuckle. The first guy had tried to be all polite southern charm with me, while the second one clearly didn't have any kind of filter.

"Okay, well, if you don't want to sit out here in the parking lot, there's an area inside where you can sit and watch us practice."

Since I was going to have to tell my entire team about what was going on now that I had two biker bodyguards following me everywhere anyway, I might as well do it now. Then, none of the team would worry whenever they saw them around me.

I couldn't help but shake my head at how fucked up my life had gotten as I walked into the large, converted warehouse that was Her Royal Hellions' home base. Before I put my skates and helmet on, I started with some stretches and warm up as I waited for the others to arrive, knowing I wouldn't have to wait long. By the time I was lacing my skates up, most of the team was there.

"What's with the hot bikers?"

I chewed my lower lip as I ran my gaze over my teammates. As much as I'd expected the women to ask, and that I knew I had to tell them, it didn't change the fact that I didn't want to confess to them about my stalker. Now that both Natalie and Nitro believed me, I was trying to let go of the worry that no one else would. But I'd been telling myself that for so long, it was hard to snap out of it. And I knew my friends would be hurt that I'd kept the secret so long from them. Her Royal Hellions were more like a family than a sports team and they were not going to be happy that I hadn't told them a long time ago. And honestly, after so many years of doing my best to keep it to myself whenever something happened, having everyone suddenly wanting to know about my past was a big mental adjustment for me.

"Ah, they would be my new bodyguards."

Silence greeted my statement. Along with a few glares and frowns.

"You know you can't leave it there. Spill, sister."

Holding Renee's gaze, I took a deep breath. I had no idea how any of them would react, but it was Renee's reaction that could make the most impact on my life. She could tell me to get out of her apartment.

"It's a bit of long story. So, ah, it turns out I have this stalker…"

For the third time in as many days, I went through all the details of my past and how this bastard had shaped my life for past eighteen years, eight months, two weeks and five days. The story rolled off my tongue easier now I'd gone over it a few times recently.

None of my derby family interrupted me, and every time I glanced up, Natalie was there giving me a smile and nod for encouragement as I spoke. When I was done, silence filled the large space. Reaching down, I adjusted my knee pads, then my elbow and wrist ones. Hoping someone would say something soon, because I had no clue what else to say.

"Holy fucking shit, Cindy! Why haven't you mentioned this asshole before now? We would have helped you."

Tears pricked my eyes and my heart swelled with love for my family. "I couldn't risk that you'd react like my mom and the police did. Ya'll are basically the only family I have left now. My aunt hates that she has to employ me and is constantly suggesting I leave. My parents moved to Florida years ago and don't visit much at all. You're all I have left. I couldn't risk losing you over this shit."

My voice cracked with emotion and I closed my eyes against the burn of tears. The next thing I knew, I was being pulled up from my seat and I found myself in the middle of a group hug.

"Never, Sin D Ella!" Renee calling me my derby name had me chuckling through my tears. "You're one of us. And actually, after hearing all of that, so much makes sense now. This stalker is why you don't date, right? Why you turn down all the Doms at the club and basically refuse all contact with men?"

I nodded as I wiped the tears from my face. "Although, it looks like Johnny—I mean Nitro—wants to brave my stalker's wrath. I don't think he's going to really give me choice about it, actually."

"Oh, is he a Dom?"

I shook my head a little. "I don't think so, at least not a trained one. He definitely has a dominant vibe going on.

He's *all* alpha male, always has been. And he spent ten years in the Navy SEALs."

The hug broke up and Renee fanned herself. "Uber protective SEAL vet, who also sounds like he may be hiding a Dom in there too. Phew, be still my heart!"

"You need to bring him to Titanium so we can all check him out while he gets run through his paces!"

"…and see how he handles Cindy's kinky side."

Within minutes we were all laughing, but inside there was a spark of fear that Nitro wouldn't accept my kinks. Not that I knew exactly what my kink was just yet, but I'd seen plenty of scenes I'd love to try out. I wasn't sure I could survive Nitro rejecting the idea. I knew I couldn't survive without Titanium. In the beginning it was simply a safe place for me to relax and work. And even though I may not have scened with a Dom yet, I'd liked what I'd seen over the years and craved to have a man take care of me like the Doms did their subs. I wanted to be able to explore my sexuality there with my friends around me. If I had to give up Titanium, it would be like slicing off a part of my heart and soul. But losing Nitro again would leave me bleeding in the same way.

"Alrighty, ladies! Enough talk, let's skate! Warm-up laps, then we'll move onto practicing blocks. I've got a couple new plays I want us to try out."

As I made my way out to the track, I shook out my shoulders and arms, forcing all thoughts from my head except for roller derby. Once on the track, I pushed off and along with my teammates, started doing laps. I loved derby, loved the skating, how free I felt when I was moving this fast. I loved how we ribbed each other and shoved at each other, the fun we had together. I was quite sure that without roller derby or Titanium, I would have gone mad years ago from the pressure of feeling like I was under a microscope most of the time.

Chapter 4

Nitro

In the week following my first lunch with Cin, nothing happened. Keys hadn't picked up anything unusual on the cameras. Jazz and Keg had been rotating guard duty after that first day, and they'd had nothing to report—well—nothing except for how hot derby chicks were. I'd also made sure I'd spoken with Cin each day and she promised me that she was being honest when she said she'd received no new notes or damage to her car. Unfortunately, none of that made her relaxed enough that she'd accept my requests for another lunch or dinner. Damn woman. Surely, she realized I wasn't going to give up until she was mine again?

I'd quietly slipped into the shop again later in the week when I knew she was working a half day and from what I observed, her aunt really didn't like her niece being there. Nor did she like Cin chatting to people who weren't paying customers. Not wanting to get her in trouble, I hadn't hung around for long.

With how she was dodging all my attempts to take her out, I was going to have to get sneaky. I was getting desperate to see her again, hopefully maybe even be able to kiss or touch her. So, determined to take Cin out to dinner, I waited until ten minutes before Retro Funk closed to arrive, then I stayed out the front of the store chatting with Jazz as I kept an eye on the door. Keg was getting some sleep so he could take the next shift. I was fairly certain she'd be left to lock up, since her aunt seemed to be the kind of person who'd make Cin do as much as she could while she sat back and bitched about it. That was something else I planned to do tonight—talk to her about why she worked for her aunt when clearly the woman didn't think much of her. I knew nothing about my girl was simple, so there had to be a story behind it. I could get Keys to dig into the history of the store to try to work it out, but I didn't want to take up any more of the man's time, especially when I could simply ask Cin for the details.

"What are you doing here? Has something happened?"

The panic lacing her voice had me muttering a curse. Maybe turning up unannounced hadn't been my best idea. Although, it wasn't like she'd left me any other options.

"Relax, everything's fine, babe. I just wanted to catch you before you took off to see if I can convince you to allow me to take you out to dinner tonight?"

Her gaze took in the street as she nervously tossed her keys between her hands. "I don't know—"

"Your stalker hasn't done anything in the week since we had lunch. I've got you protected, Cin. Stop letting this bastard control your life. Unless, you really don't want me?"

With a curse she threw her head back and closed her eyes for a moment. Then she shifted so she could look me straight in the eye.

"Fine. Dinner. But I have derby practice first, I can't miss it."

From what I'd seen so far, the girl practiced just about every damn day, she was dedicated, that's for sure. And I knew it was all that practice that made her so damn good at it. I'd been on their website and done some Googling. My girl rocked on skates. Moving forward, I snagged the hand not currently holding her keys, and pulled her against me, pressing a kiss to her temple while I enjoyed the hell out of having her body pressed up against mine. Even if we were both clothed. Later, I'd fix that.

"I know, Cin. I wouldn't ever ask you to skip something you love. I'm gonna come watch you in action, see what all the fuss is about, then we'll head out to eat."

She opened her mouth, frowned, then with a shake of her head pulled away from me and proceeded to lock up the front door of the shop.

"I need to go home and get changed first. Did you bring your bike, or do you want to come with me?"

The fact she hadn't really tried to get out of dinner had my hopes for the evening rising. I couldn't resist pulling her back against me, cupping her face and putting my mouth against hers, when she'd finished locking up. I'd missed this woman so fucking much and I couldn't wait to reacquaint myself with every inch of her. To drown myself in her taste.

"I'll follow you back to your place, then we'll go together."

As much as I'd fucking love to have her on the back of my bike, I wasn't sure if that would be possible with her in her derby gear. However, I didn't have a problem with being caged in her car if it meant I got to be close to her.

She glanced at Jazz briefly before looking back to me. "And since you're with me, do I still need the bodyguard?"

"Yeah, babe, you do. Because I know full well I'm going to be totally focused on you tonight, not watching what's going on around us, Jazz is gonna be guarding both our backs. Until we catch this fucker, I'm not taking any risks with your safety."

Well, that wasn't completely true. I would be keeping watch of what was going on around us, but I wasn't sending away my back-up. The more people watching out for my woman, the safer she would be.

"You'll have Keg after practice. We'll switch out while she's safely inside the warehouse."

I gave Jazz a nod before all three of us started walking toward the parking lot. Reluctantly, I gave Cin another quick kiss before I left her to get into her car while I got on my bike and started it up. While she got herself sorted in her car, I took in the lot. There weren't many other cars, which was to be expected at this hour of the day, and I couldn't see anyone hanging around. It had only been a week but not being able to catch this fucker was already wearing on my nerves. It had to be someone from Bridgewater, someone who had known her as a teen well enough to grow fixated on her. And young enough that nearly nineteen years later he was still able to bother her. I mentally ran through all the people I could think of but couldn't come up with anyone who I didn't still see around town regularly. I needed to ask Keys if he could somehow find out who else moved to Houston around the same time Cin did, or who often visited Houston. It was probably near impossible to determine but I figured it was worth a shot. The man often pulled miracles out of his computer.

A few minutes later, Jazz and I followed Cindy's car through the gates in the apartment building's parking garage that had opened automatically. I was grateful her building had such good security for its parking. Not only did it decrease the chances of her car getting screwed with again, it meant my bike would be safe while I was with her too. After pulling up next to Jazz in the space beside her car, I turned off my ride and swung my leg over the seat. I wanted to see where she lived. I also wanted to spend the night with her here tonight, but didn't want to get my hopes up too much just yet on that front.

"I just need to change quickly and grab my bag. Did you want to—"

I cut her off before she could imply I'd stay here in the damn garage. "I'd love to see where you live, babe, I promise I won't do anything that'll make you late to practice."

By the stiff way Cin walked off I could tell she wasn't happy. The silent treatment she was throwing my way was another pretty good clue to her current mood. And made me feel like a bastard for railroading her. When we came to a stop in front of the elevator, I spoke up.

"If you really don't want me to come up with you, I can go hang with Jazz."

With a sigh, her body relaxed and she shook her head before turning to face me.

"It's not that I don't want you with me. It's just—you're taking this bodyguard thing too far. This building is well protected. I've never received anything from him here."

The elevator doors opening cut off whatever else she was going to say. I followed her in, and once she pressed the button for her floor and before she could speak again, I pulled her in against me and pressed a kiss to the top of her head.

"Babe, you're not on your own anymore. I'm here for you, not as your bodyguard but as your damn man. I'll always be here for you. I would have been here for you the whole time if I'd known where the fuck you were and what was going on. I'm not here only to find this fucker stalking you, I'm here for you. To spend time with you. To learn about who you are now. And that includes getting a look at where you live."

Her head fell forward against my chest as she slipped her hands under my cut. The thin t-shirt I had on did nothing to ease the burning trail her fingers left as she slipped her arms around my waist to hold me against her. Leaning down, I rested my cheek against the top of her head as I wrapped my arms around her. A shudder ran through me at how right it felt to hold her like this. It was peaceful and, well, it was simply fucking perfect.

I just managed to not growl when she pulled away after the elevator dinged and the doors opened. I could have stayed like that forever. At least she seemed to be just as reluctant as me to end the contact and when she reached for my hand, I followed her lead, tightening my grip on her to make sure she didn't drop my hand as we headed toward her apartment.

Once through the door I was a little shocked at what I found. The apartment was nice, but it was all super modern, sleek with sharp clean lines. I'd expected Cin to have little things sitting all over the place. If the way she now dressed was any indication, she hadn't lost her love for all things old and funky.

"So, the apartment is really Renee's place. She'd lived here for a few years before I moved in and I didn't have much, so I have my room, which has its own bathroom thankfully, and that's about it, really."

She sounded flustered and nervous, so I let the subject drop. But it didn't stop my heart clenching at how sad it was that she'd lived here for over ten years yet still only had one room that she could call her own. Back in Bridgewater, I had a room at the clubhouse and a house near the bar but I'd never done much with the place. Cin would have a field day decorating it and putting her stamp all over it, I was sure. And I couldn't wait for the day to arrive when she was living with me and able to do just that.

I hoped like fuck that because she hadn't been able to make herself at home here, that I wouldn't have too hard a time convincing her to move in with me. I wasn't sure how attached she was to her job at Titanium, but I doubted she'd miss having to work with her aunt if she moved to Bridgewater. The drive from there to Houston wasn't so long that she'd have to give up her derby team. I knew she wouldn't budge on that one, and she shouldn't have to. I'd never expect her to give up on her dreams. Although, it would probably help if I could find her somewhere local to practice at least a couple nights a week so she wasn't driving up here every day.

As soon as I entered her room, I didn't even try to hold back my grin. Now *this* was what I expected from my girl. The room wasn't messy so much as it was cluttered with more stuff than really fit. There were little knick-knack and trinket filled shelves against the walls and a small desk with a closed laptop and more retro looking trinkets covering its surface. The bed was made up with what looked like a handmade patchwork quilt. Maybe something her grandma had made?

She cleared her throat. "Sorry about the mess. Renee is a clean freak so I've learned to be careful in the rest of the house, but in here I like things more, ah, artfully arranged."

Her cheeks flushed and I couldn't resist. With a chuckle I stepped up close to her and wrapped one palm around the back of her neck while I used the other one to tilt her chin up.

"Out there isn't you at all, but in here? This is you, it feels and smells like you and I love it."

Before she could say a word, I took her mouth in a deep, passionate kiss. It took all my control to pull back, to stop before we ended up naked on her bed with me balls deep inside her. Didn't mean I was happy about having to stop, and I may have growled a little.

"Hurry up and change, babe. Not sure how long I can resist the urge to strip you down and fuck you hard, like I'm dying to do."

She blinked up at me in shock for a moment, then seemed to shake herself back to reality and with a little gasp, dashed toward her closet where she started pulling out clothing. Realizing if I watched her strip to get changed, I really would throw her on the bed, I turned my back toward her and began to examine some of her little trinkets as I tried to not listen to the rustle of clothing as she changed.

Cindy

Having Johnny with me as I went through my everyday routine had me on cloud nine. He'd seemed a little uncomfortable in the car on the way to the warehouse, but I figured that was probably just a biker thing. Once at practice, I'd had a job and a half to keep the other girls focused on derby. I think they all would have preferred to spend the session grilling Johnny about our past rather than doing laps or any of the other things we were supposed to be focusing on at the moment.

Johnny had been the perfect spectator. He silently stood to the side of the track and watched. I knew he'd had eyes only for me because I'd been able to feel them on me, burning into my skin the entire time I'd skated. I somehow managed to not crash out, but it had been a close call more than once.

Now I was freshly showered, changed and heading out of the warehouse holding his hand, I couldn't help but smile. This was such a nice, normal thing to do but something I hadn't done in a very long time.

"You girls really get into it, huh?"

"Yep, we practice as we compete. I love it."

He chuckled. "I can tell. Guess it's a great way to blow off steam too."

"Sure is, but it's more than that. I found a family when I joined the Hellions. I wouldn't have survived so long without them."

"That I get. I feel the same way about the Charons. After you left, well, I kinda went off the rails. It was a couple of the older brothers who pulled me aside and made sure I didn't blow my chance with the Navy, or with life in general. I have no idea where I'd be if they hadn't done what they did for me back then, or the hundreds of times since."

My stomach twisted into knots at the reminder that my actions, or rather the actions forced on me by my stalker, hadn't just affected my own life, but Nitro's too.

"I really am sorry, Nitro. I didn't want to leave you but I didn't want you hurt either, so I did the only thing I thought I could."

Had I made a mistake all those years ago in running away? Maybe I should have told him then what was going on. Although, since then he'd been through the SEALs and was now part of a dangerous MC. He had all sorts of skills and back-up now that he hadn't had back then.

I was pulled from my thoughts when he stopped and crushed me against him in a tight embrace.

"Let it all go, babe. It was a long time ago, and there's nothing we can do about the past. Just promise me you won't keep secrets from me going forward. Whatever happens from here on out, we'll handle it together. Okay?"

Tears pricked my eyes but I blinked them away, refusing to let any of them fall. "That sounds wonderful." I paused to clear my throat. "So, where are we off to for dinner?"

"Hand over the keys, and you'll soon find out."

I'd known he would say that—even as a teenager he'd liked to be in control. He really was like the Doms at Titanium. As we got settled in my car and he revved the engine, I got lost in thought, thinking about how Nitro would react to the club. I figured it could go one of two ways. He'd either accept it and the fact I worked there, or he'd reject it completely and lose his shit that I worked in such a place. Fuck, I hoped he accepted it. Who was I kidding? I was hoping for more than just acceptance, I wanted him to be willing to try it with me. How would it feel to have Johnny, or rather Nitro, spanking me? A hot flash of arousal blasted through my body and brought me out of my daydream. Licking my lips, I slipped a glance at Nitro, relief coursing through me when it looked like he hadn't noticed I was sitting here getting horny as hell from my little daydream about him.

He was looking straight ahead and had his full attention focused on the road. That was something he used to do too, always taking such care when he was driving. While he was busy, I took the time to really look at him. He'd certainly filled out over the years—his muscles were bigger, his shoulders broader. His square jawline was the same hard line that I'd loved to press kisses over, but the scruff over it was new. He'd always been clean shaven back in school. There was a slight touch of gray in the scruff and at his temples, too. His hair looked like it was as soft as it had always been and my fingers twitched with my desire to feel it again. As I took in his muscular frame, I wondered if he had any ink. Surely he would. Between the Navy and the MC, he'd have to have at least some, right?

"I can feel you staring at me, babe. What's on your mind?"

"Just wondering if you have any ink."

His lips ticked up into a sexy grin. "Yeah, I got ink, babe. How about I show you later, and then you can show me all of yours?"

I barked out a laugh at his antics. "Ah, yes, the old 'You show me yours, I'll show you mine.' I see your lines haven't changed much."

He'd said that to me when I'd gotten nervous the first time we'd been together. It was stupid and corny, but it had made me laugh and smoothed the way for the rest of the evening. The car slowed as he pulled into a parking space, he shut the engine off then turned his full attention to me.

"I wasn't sure you'd remember. And I promise you, you are the only one I've ever said that to."

Like I'd ever forget anything about the night I gave him my virginity. Unable to resist any longer, I lifted my hand and scraped my nails over his jaw, through his scruff. The short hairs tickled against my skin. With a low growl, he leaned in to me, I took his hint, and threading my fingers through his silky soft hair, lifted my face to his to accept another of his delicious kisses.

His lips slid over mine, gentle for a moment before he pressed closer and deepened the kiss. Feeling like a flower in the sun after the rain, I opened up for him, dancing my tongue with his. He tasted the same as he always had, and as my senses filled with it my mind spun back to when we'd first gotten together. To the first time he'd kissed me. It had been at school during lunch, he'd pulled me behind a couple of trees so we were out of sight, then he'd wrapped his palm around the back of my neck, tilted my face up with the other hand and took my mouth. It was a memory that I'd dreamed of often over the years, and it was a dream that always left me craving him once I woke.

"Baby, what's wrong?"

He'd pulled back from the kiss and I blinked up at him, wondering what he meant, until he ran his thumbs over my cheeks, wiping away tears I hadn't realized I'd been shedding. My sudden issues with leaking all the time were becoming annoying. I wasn't a crier normally, and I didn't like being one now. Not that I could do much about it in this moment, not with him sitting there looking all worried and being so damn sweet.

"I missed you. So much."

His hold on my face tightened for a moment.

"Fuck, babe. All these years, there hasn't been a single fucking day I haven't thought of you, dreamed of you."

"It's been the same for me."

With a growl, he gave me a fast, hard kiss that left me stunned silent for a moment when he tore himself away.

"Tell me we can skip dinner—tell me we can go back to your place and order something in. I need you, Cin."

Warmth flooded my system as my mouth went dry. Holding his gaze, I nodded as I couldn't seem to get any words out.

After flashing me with a broad grin filled with promise, he turned back to face the dash and started the car. He pulled out of the parking lot, the tires squealing as he sped off down the road.

Nerves weaved through my arousal as we got closer to my apartment. I hadn't had sex with anyone since Johnny. It had been a long damn time since anyone had seen me naked, touched me. I had a good collection of toys but that wasn't the same. And while I'd stayed celibate, I was quite certain he had not. I knew most MCs had women at their clubhouses who were there for the sole purpose of fucking the men. Had he used women like that? Would he want someone as inexperienced as me? My arousal cooled off as more questions and worries swirled around my mind. Was this a mistake? Maybe we should have stuck with eating out somewhere.

Chapter 5

Nitro

I had no fucking idea what had changed between leaving the restaurant parking lot and arriving at Cin's place, but something had. She'd been as hot as I'd been before we left, but now she'd gone cold. She sat staring out the windshield, chewing on her bottom lip like she was trying to solve the world's problems by herself tonight.

"C'mon, babe. Let's go up and order some food."

I wanted her more than my next breath, but I wasn't going to force things. It'd been a long time since we were last together. I knew we needed to take a little time to reconnect, that it would be better holding off until we did talk a bit more. Hopefully sharing a meal in the comfort of her apartment would be enough for her to accept me. Or at least tell me what the fuck had happened on the drive over.

I got out and went around to open her door for her, but she'd beat me to it. She'd just swung her legs out but hadn't stood up yet. I looked down into her eyes and my gut clenched at the pain in her eyes. Crouching down in front of her, I took her hands in mine.

"Cindy, nothing has to happen tonight you don't want. We'll head up, order in a pizza or something, chat and catch up. If things get heated again, that's great—if not, that's fine too. Okay?"

Although, it wouldn't be easy to be in her house, her bedroom, surrounded by her things with her scent in the air and not be naked with her, to be able to touch her all over. Fuck, I'd give just about anything to be able to make love to my Cin again.

Slowly, I stood and pulled her up out of the seat. Once her door was shut, I locked the car up, and not releasing my hold on her hand, I led her over to the elevator. As soon as the doors slid shut, closing us inside, she cleared her throat.

"So, ah, are there women at the Charon MC clubhouse?"

I frowned as I tried to work out what she was really asking.

"Sure. Some of the brothers are married and their old ladies come around sometimes."

"Old ladies?"

Why did so many women have such an issue with that damn title?

"It's not a derogatory term, Cin. An old lady is a brother's wife, or partner. They also wear their man's property patch. Again, it's not a derogatory thing. Quite the opposite. It's a sign of respect, to be the old lady of a brother and to wear his property patch means you're part of the club. That the entire club has accepted you into its ranks and every one of them will have your back if anything happens. Makes you family, protected and cherished."

She shook her head and stayed quiet as we moved from the elevator, down the hall and into her apartment. I let her lead the way and followed her as she moved into the living area and sat on a couch. My ass had barely hit the seat beside her when she started up the conversation again.

"But I'm not your old lady and the club is helping me. What does that make me?"

Fuck it all. How do I explain this in a way she won't kick me out for pushing her too hard, too fast?

I turned so I was facing her, and took her hand between both of mine as I looked her directly in the eye.

"You grew up in Bridgewater, Cin, you know the stories that float around about the club and what they've done in the past. Most of that is based on truth. Doesn't matter who you are, old lady, club whore, even if you were a complete stranger to the club—if the Charon MC got word of what you'd been living through, that the cops were ignoring the whole thing, they'd have stepped up to deal with it."

Her eyes hardened and I tried not to squirm under her intense stare.

"I've never heard of the club taking care of a perfect stranger, and I'm not sure I like the sounds of the other option. What the fuck is a club whore?"

Yeah, I should have known I'd fuck up that explanation where I tried to leave out the important shit. But since there was no way in hell I was going to stand for her thinking she was a fucking club whore, looked like I was going to have to lay it all out and hope like fuck she didn't boot me out the door at the end.

"You will never be a club whore, Cindy. They are women who hang around the clubhouse for the sole purpose of meeting the brothers' sexual needs. Those women choose to be there for that very purpose, they know what is expected of them before they come in." I paused to take a deep breath as I hoped she took what I was about to tell her the right way. "Like I mentioned earlier, after you left, I went wild. Stopped caring about pretty much every damn thing. And it was a few of the Charons who took me aside and got me to calm my shit down enough that I didn't blow my chances at the SEALs. That's how I first got involved with the Charons."

I paused to take another deep breath. Nerves were tearing up my gut. How was she going to react?

"Part of their offer to help me was that I needed to come clean about what was going on with my life. So Scout and Bulldog, they're now the club's president and vice president, know all about who you are to me. They know I ain't ever letting you get away from me again. So,

Cin, you see, as far as the club is concerned, you're already my old lady. I just haven't put a patch on your back yet."

I was actually fairly certain Scout would have ordered her cut already. He seemed to do that whenever a brother started to get serious about a woman. Cindy had a sheen of tears over her eyes but she didn't let them fall as she bit her lower lip and continued to hold my gaze.

"I've been alone so long now, it's hard to wrap my head around all of this. To believe it."

Leaning forward, I scooped her up and put her on my lap.

"I know, babe. I wish we could go back and fix this shit when it first started, but since that's not possible, we'll fix it now. Then we can focus on us and setting up our future together."

She gave me a small nod before her gaze dropped to my mouth. When she licked her lips I was done for. Gently wrapping my palm around the back of her neck, I held her still as I took her mouth with mine. On a groan, she opened up for me and I took the invitation, allowing our tongues to dance and play as I slipped one palm down her body to cup her breast. With a groan of my own, I pinched the tip through her clothes and enjoyed the fuck out of the way she shuddered against me.

Disappointment crashed through me when she pulled away, but I didn't try to stop her. I was desperately trying to not push her past her comfort zone. Even if it was going to leave me with the worst case of blue balls I'd ever had, we would do this at her pace. With her gaze cast downward, she slipped off my lap and stood.

"Renee'll be home soon. C'mon."

Unsure whether she was kicking me out or inviting me to her room, I held my breath as I stood and followed her. Relief flooded me when she turned toward her room. By the time we made it to the doorway, my cock was as hard as steel, ready and hoping things were going to go the way it wanted them to. With a forced calm, I closed the door firmly, before turning to face her. She was so fucking adorable. Clearly, she was nervous as hell, but before I could say a word, she was on me, slamming herself against my front so fast she nearly bounced off, but I was quick to wrap my arms around her to hold her against me.

"Please, Johnny, make me feel again. Kiss me, touch me, fuck me—"

I cut off her words with a shake of my head. I couldn't stand her thinking I would simply be fucking her. It would never be like that with Cin, it couldn't be when I loved her as much as I did. "I'll be loving you, Cindy. I'll do all that and more, but it'll be because I fucking love you, always have and always will."

The way she'd spoken, it had sounded like she had an itch she needed scratched, and I wasn't going to stand for that. Not from her. She was fucking mine, not some random chick I was banging because I was hard. So, she'd better be doing this because I was hers too. Not just because she was horny and I was handy.

Her expression softened and when a single tear slipped down her right cheek, I lifted my thumb to brush it away as my gut tightened in fear that I'd just done what I swore I wouldn't and pushed her too much.

"Ever since I left, there's been this hole in my world. It sounds so stupid, but I don't know how else to explain it. I've tried to fill my life with work and roller derby, friends, Titanium. But nothing's worked. I'm still lonely, I still miss you, Johnny. I miss what we had. I know it can't be exactly like that now, we're not teenagers anymore, but that bond we had? That can be the same, can't it? Do you think we can find that again?"

She didn't say she loved me, but that was okay. She'd said a lot of other things that were pretty damn close to it, and she'd told me once a long time ago, so I knew I could earn it from her again.

"We can. We totally can. Now, say you're mine."

My voice was little more than a growl, and I fucking loved how her body melted against mine in response.

"I'm yours. Only yours."

As she spoke, I wrapped my hand in her hair to tilt her head back so I could kiss her again. I fucking loved her mouth, her taste. But I kept the kiss short because as much as I wanted to keep kissing her mouth, I wanted to get my lips on other parts of her I'd been missing too.

"Need you naked, Cin."

"Hmmm."

She didn't say anything else as she stepped back and reached for the bottom of her shirt. She might not have said a word, but the way she paused and raised an eyebrow at me, made it pretty clear what she wanted. With a grin, I shrugged out of my cut, draping it over a chair before I reached over my head to grab the back of my shirt to pull it off. Once it was gone, I looked back to Cin and groaned. Then, I nearly fell to my fucking knees in front of her. She was even sexier now than she'd been as a teenager. Her curves had filled out perfectly, and all the exercise she did showed in the lean lines of her muscles.

Cindy

Here in my bedroom, he wasn't Nitro. Nope, here he was my Johnny, and when he slipped off his vest then reached for his shirt, I gladly followed his lead, shedding my own shirt along with my bra as fast as I could manage. But then I stalled out. Out of reflex, my palms rose to cover my boobs as I stood frozen to the spot, staring at what he revealed as he twisted to dump his clothes on a chair, followed by his boots.

He had more ink than me, between the tattoos on his shoulders and the huge one on his back. He was so big now, all sinewy muscle and, well, fucking perfection. He'd filled out considerably since his teen years and had reached the potential I'd known he would.

But what would he think of me? I was fit and lean thanks to all the exercise I got with derby but I wasn't perfect. My butt jiggled, my boobs were bigger and they sagged a little now. Just as I neared a full on panic attack, he turned around and the look on his face, the groan he made, gave me the boost my confidence desperately needed at that precise moment.

"Drop your hands, baby. Let me see you."

Every word he said reminded me of things I'd overheard Doms say to their subs at Titanium. It raised my hopes that he'd react positively when we went to Titanium. Maybe with Johnny by my side, I could finally get out from behind the bar and join in. Stop being a damn spectator.

Him prowling toward me had me dropping all other thoughts that were running around my head and backing away. My knees hitting the bed forced me stop, and with a dangerously sexy grin, he dropped to his knees in front of me. With one palm sliding around my thigh, then over my ass and up my back, his other cupped my breast, while his mouth latched onto the remaining nipple. I locked my knees when they threatened to give out and slipped my hands into his hair. The suction of his hot mouth and the pinch of his fingers had wave after wave of arousal crashing through my body.

He switched things over so both sides got the full treatment, and by the time he released me a second time, I was nearly mindless with desire. He nuzzled his face against the underside of my boobs while his fingers worked at the zipper of my skirt. His big palms slipped underneath and pushed the material down, revealing the lacy panties, garter belt and stockings I'd put back on after derby practice. I wore them for work to go with the pin-up outfit, but normally after practice I left the stockings and garter belt off. However, tonight I'd been hoping we'd end up here like this so I'd taken the time to put them back on. And I was glad I had when he lightly flicked one of the garter straps.

"Cin, this get-up is sexy as fuck, babe. You wear this under those pin-up clothes every day?"

"Pretty much. Why?"

Cupping my ass in his palms, he pulled me forward as he buried his face between my breasts with a groan.

"Because it's going to be even harder to not jump you every time I see you dressed like that now I know." He pulled back enough to stand. "Got a really good feeling we're gonna get real inventive at finding places for me to have you during the day."

That left me grinning. "Nothing new there, babe."

He laughed, as I'd wanted him to do. As teenagers both living at home, we'd had to get creative to find places we could have enough privacy to have sex. Before I could say anything else, he picked me up and tossed me onto my bed.

"Johnny!"

He just smirked at me before he frowned at my waist area.

"Babe, can't tell you how much I fucking love that get-up, but I've got no clue how to get your panties off without just ripping them off."

With a gasp of horror I shook my head and glared at him. "Don't you dare start ripping my underwear! This shit's expensive."

Reaching down, I made fast work of unclipping my stockings and undoing the garter belt. As I pulled it off, Johnny reached over and peeled my panties down my legs, knocking my shoes to the floor in the process. When he stood back up, I was left wearing nothing but my unclipped stockings.

"You trust me to take these off, babe?"

I nodded and kept my gaze on him as he very carefully slid first one stocking down, then the other. His callused fingers caressed my skin as he moved and shivers wracked my body when he pressed a gentle kiss to the arch of my foot.

"So fucking beautiful, babe."

With my heart in my throat, I slowly lifted my gaze to look up into his face, almost unable to believe what was happening. What I was hearing. Needing to touch him, I reached a hand up, cupping his face as he leaned forward over me.

"Tell me I'm not dreaming right now. Promise me this is real."

Turning his face, he kissed my palm before he pulled back to nip at my fingertips.

"This is a fucking dream come true, Cin. I promise you're wide awake right now, baby, and no fucking alarm clock is gonna go off and destroy this."

Then he released my hand and dropped to kneel beside the bed. Before I could work out what he was doing, he gripped my ankles and pulled me until my butt was on the edge of the mattress.

"Johnny!"

Before I could get another word out, my breath caught as he ran his palms up my inner thighs, spreading me wider for him. Exposing me completely to his hot gaze.

"Ohhh!"

His tongue swiped up my center and jolts of electricity shot through my body, short-circuiting my brain. His growl was my only warning before he settled his mouth over my pussy and thrust his tongue in deep. It was more sensation than I'd felt in forever and I couldn't help but try to get away from it, even though him stopping was the last thing I wanted. With another sexy growl, he gripped my hips and held me down as he went back to making a meal out of me.

I fisted both hands in the bedding as my head thrashed, already on the verge of coming. I tried to hold it off, not wanting him to stop so soon. He'd learned some tricks since we'd last been in this position, and I wanted more of his nibbling, sucking and licking before I gave in.

"Fuck, Cin. Give it to me, stop holding back."

He only lifted away from me long enough to speak, then he was back at me, sucking on my clit as he thrust two fingers up inside me, finding that one spot, and then it was all over. With a scream, I climaxed harder than I think I ever had before.

My brain cleared to discover my body still trembling and the sight of Johnny stripping out of his socks and jeans.

"Hmmm. You still have the sexiest ass."

He looked over his shoulder at me with a smirk, as he dropped his jeans on the chair with the rest of his clothes.

"Glad you like what you see, babe. Scoot up the bed for me?"

Taking a deep breath for strength, I managed to roll over and start crawling up the bed. I hadn't gone very far when Johnny wrapped an arm around my middle, scooting me up higher as his other hand hit the bed near my shoulder and his big body covered mine. His soft lips trailed kisses over my shoulder and up my neck before I turned my face so he could kiss me again. I loved how he kissed me, as if he wanted to inhale me with each one. The slight tang of my cream on his tongue did nothing but heighten my arousal.

A small squeak escaped me when he released his hold on me so he could flip me around so I was on my back, beneath him.

"As much as I love taking you from behind, and fully intend to later, I want to look into your eyes this first time."

Glancing down, I got my first look at his cock. Had that gotten bigger too? I wasn't sure, and I sure as hell wasn't going to ask! He was hard, thick and long. And he'd already put a condom on. I wanted to touch and taste and relearn him like he'd done me, but I guessed that would just have to wait until later. Because even though I'd only just come, the need to feel him inside me again was strong. It had been forever, —well, technically it had been eighteen years, eight months- My thoughts broke off and heat filled my face when I looked back up to his face, catching his smug expression at my blatant ogling of his body.

"Looks like you're all wrapped and ready to go, so what are you waiting for, sailor?"

"Don't push me, Cindy. I've been waiting for this for nearly nineteen fucking years. I ain't gonna rush it."

I ran my palms up his arms, leaving them resting on his shoulders when he took hold of his cock and lined the head up with my entrance. My body began trembling when the slight burn hit as he pressed in, stretching me. My grip on his shoulders slipped until my palms were back on the bedding, reaching for fists full of anything to grip onto. My eyes blurred but it wasn't pain that had me tearing up, but joy. Happiness twisted with the arousal flowing through my body as I took Johnny inside me for the first time in eighteen years, eight months, three weeks and five days. Not that I'd been counting.

Blinking clear the moisture, I took in his face as he watched where we were joined. His expression was so damn sexy. He looked completely enthralled with what he was seeing, so I followed his gaze. I'd lasered all the hair from my pussy years ago, so there was nothing to impede the sight of his thick length disappearing inside my core before sliding back out again. The mix of the visual along with the pressure of taking him inside me after so long left me whimpering and wanting more.

Chapter 6

Nitro

Watching Cin take my cock inside her was a moment I'd never forget. She was so fucking tight, her channel clenched against my length as I fought my way inside her pussy. I took it slow, easing in a little, then pulling back some before I entered again a little deeper. Part of me wanted to rush, wanted to slam inside of her and claim what was mine, but the other, larger part of me, knew we had all fucking night to enjoy this. And I really didn't want to hurt her, especially like this. She was so damn tight that I didn't doubt the truth that she truly hadn't taken another man inside her since she'd left me. Made me feel like a fucking bastard for all the women I'd fucked over the years, but I hadn't known she was out there waiting for me. And now I could use all those skills I'd learned for her benefit, to make her mine again. I would never leave my woman wanting.

Once I was buried balls deep, I paused to absorb the sensation of being surrounded by her heat, and to give her a moment to adjust to my size. After a few moments,

I leaned over her and took her mouth, kissing her with all the desperation and passion I was feeling. *Fuck*, but I wanted to inhale her. Her hands came up to rest on my hips as she began to squirm beneath me.

"You ready for more, Cin?"

"Please."

"Love you, Cin."

I whispered the words against her lips before I kissed her again while I pulled my pelvis back and thrust into her. Her fingers dug into my sides and she broke the kiss with a gasp and arch of her back. I lifted my body up off her as I continued to move in and out of her. The only thing that would make this better was if I wasn't wearing a fucking condom. I'd give my Harley to be able to take her bareback, to have the right to fill her womb with my seed.

One day.

Make that one day soon, I'd make it so I had that right as quickly as possible. Cindy Davis was mine. The only woman for me.

Gripping one of her legs, I lifted it up high as I ground against her, making sure I brushed over her clit before I began thrusting in and out again, deeper this time.

"Johnny!"

Fuck it all, but I loved how she said my name in a breathy scream when I did something that surprised her. I couldn't remember the last time someone had called me Johnny. Probably my folks, before I left for BUD/S training. But the way Cin said it just now? Best fucking sound in the world.

A sheen of sweat coated her skin as she arched again and started to buck and wriggle against me.

"Whatcha want, babe?"

"More! Harder, faster… I need you. More."

The desperation in her wide, desire-soaked gaze had me feeling ten feet tall. After quickly leaning in to kiss her again, I kneeled between her legs and took hold of her hips so I could pound into her hard and fast like she wanted. Within a few strokes, a tingle shot down my spine and my balls drew up, ready to blow. Shifting one hand, I gave her clit a tweak and pinch. That was all it took—she screamed out as she came. Her pussy clenched tight around me, forcing me over the edge with her. I couldn't hold back the roar that erupted as I came deep inside my woman.

With the last jerk of my cock inside her, I dropped over her as I attempted to catch my breath. I nuzzled my face in against her neck and pressed a kiss to the soft skin there. Her arms came up around my shoulders and I rolled us to the side so I wouldn't crush her under my weight. We stayed like that for a few minutes. I didn't want to fucking move but I needed to deal with the condom.

Reluctantly, I pulled back from her and slid off the bed.

"Back in a sec."

I quickly ducked into the bathroom that was attached to her bedroom, disposed of the condom, and wet a cloth before returning to her. She lay just as I'd left her, her eyes barely open and a slightly goofy grin on her face. She looked like a well-satisfied woman, a fact that had me standing a little taller as I strode over to her. Gently lifting her leg, I cleaned her inner thighs and pussy before moving to toss the cloth in the sink in the bathroom, then I turned off the bedroom light and came back to her.

Scooping her off the bed, I held her against me with one arm, as I shoved the bedding back. Then I placed her gently down before I slipped onto the mattress to lie beside her. As I reached to draw her in against me, she pulled the covers up over us.

"Get some rest, babe, because that was just the warm-up."

She chuckled and wriggled until her back was tight up against my front. Warmth filled my heart when I wrapped my arm around her and cupped her breast in my palm and she sighed and relaxed further against me. This is what I'd been missing all these years, craving. Having Cin like this, content and safe in my arms.

Cindy

I stood in the kitchen, waiting for the pod machine to heat up as Johnny showered. Thankfully I didn't have to be anywhere until later in the day and Renee had already left for work. Johnny made love to me three more times during the night so this morning I was feeling sore, but I wasn't about to start complaining. Nope. In fact, I couldn't wait to do it all again tonight. That thought had me chewing my lip in concern. I was working at Titanium tonight, so if Johnny wanted to hang with me, I needed to tell him about what kind of club it was before he walked into the place.

He came up behind me and wrapped his arms around my middle, pulling me back against him as he pressed a kiss to the top of my head.

"What has you looking so worried, babe?"

"I need to tell you something, and I'm not sure how you're going to react."

He tensed up behind me just as the first cup finished filling. He loosened his hold so I could switch out the pods and put a second cup in to be filled with coffee. Once I was done, I turned to hand him his.

"I assume you still take it black, no sugar?"

He was frowning as he nodded and took the mug from my hand. I grabbed my own brew before heading for the couch. He sat beside me and set his mug on the coffee table before twisting so he was facing me directly.

"Just spit it out, babe. Nothing you can say will change how I feel about you. You know that, right?"

"In theory." I took a mouthful of my coffee before I set it beside his and faced him. "What do you know about the club, Titanium?"

"I know you work the bar there. Why?"

"So you don't know what kind of club it is?"

His frown deepened as he stared at me intently. "I hope you're not about to tell me you work at a strip club. Because if that's the case, you'll be quitting."

I couldn't help it, I burst out laughing. "You're part of an MC that keeps a bunch of whores on the payroll, and you're going to throw shade at a strip club? That's rich. And don't MCs own most of the strip clubs around the country, anyhow?"

He actually growled at me. "Don't give a fuck what other clubs do. The Charons don't own one, and even if we did, I still wouldn't have my woman working there."

I patted his knee. "Take a breath, it's not a strip club. Now, I seriously do only work behind the bar, so don't get upset. Titanium is a kink club." He sat silently, looking blankly at me. "You know? BDSM? Fifty shades and all that stuff? Do I really have to explain that to you? You've never spanked a girl's butt?"

He seemed caught in a brain freeze or something, and it was scaring the shit out of me. I mean, if he was so judgey over the thought of me working in a strip club, what the fuck would he really think of a kink club? I went on the defensive, trying to make him understand.

"Natalie, the captain of Her Royal Hellions, owns the club. It's all very high class and not sleazy at all. After my Grandma died and my Aunt Skye took over Retro Funk, she cut my hours back, and I needed another job. When I asked my derby family about it, Natalie said she needed a good bartender at Titanium. She did say I could play at the club too, around my work hours of course, but I never have. I couldn't risk it with, well, you know. And I know at this point I'm rambling but your strong and silent routine is starting to freak me the fuck out. Please, tell me what you're thinking."

He reached out and grabbed my hands in his.

"I've got no fucking clue what to say to that, Cin. I've never been in a club like that to know what goes on inside one. So, it's some kind of sex club? Is that what you're saying?"

I shook my head. "No, it's not like that. I mean, sure, sex happens but it's not orgies and stuff. And there's privacy rooms where people go to have sex. That doesn't happen out on the floor. It's not allowed. There are lots of rules that everyone has to follow, it's very safe. To be honest, I doubt my stalker has been able to gain access. I probably could have played there without—"

I stopped talking when he growled at me.

"Gah, stop doing that! You're not a damn dog! Use your words. If you start talking, I'll stop rambling. You know how I get when I'm nervous."

He tugged my hands until I shifted so I was sitting across his lap.

"I don't like the idea of you *playing* with other men, Cin. That shit'll have me growling at you every damn time. Am I allowed in this place? To see what really fucking goes on in there?"

I lifted my palm to his face where I ran my short nails through his scruff, trying to calm the beast.

"I'll need to double check with Natalie, but I'm pretty sure you will be. Normally new members have to fill out forms and stuff before they're allowed in. But since I need to go in a little early to set up, we might be able to get you to fill everything out while I'm doing that."

Johnny reached over me to grab his coffee while I pulled my phone out and shot a text off to Natalie.

"Since I'm working tonight, you can sit at the bar and keep me company while you watch what goes on. Wednesday nights aren't as busy as later in the week."

"How many nights do you work?"

"Normally four nights a week. Wednesday through Saturday, then on Sunday afternoon I go in for a few hours. Natalie holds training sessions on Sundays and there's food and drinks available for attendees. But I don't have to work that much, it's only because I want to that I do. Now that you're back in my life, I'll see about cutting back my nights. If you want?"

Although less work would be less pay, I'd managed to put a little away over the years so I could survive working a little less for a while.

"Let's see how tonight goes, I don't want to upend your entire life, babe. But once we get this stalker situation dealt with, we'll need to decide what we're going to do. I run the club's bar back in Bridgewater. The others are taking care of it while I take care of you, but I'll need to get back to it at some point. You have a job there too, if you want it. I'd also fucking love it if you'd move back to Bridgewater with me. How many times a week do you train for derby?"

My breath stuttered in my chest. This was all getting very heavy, extremely quickly. Move back to Bridgewater? To live with Nitro? After a couple deep breaths, I pushed that side of what he said away and focused on derby.

"Personally, I train every day. We have to go to two training sessions each week. One with the league and one with the team. The other nights it's low key and is just whoever turns up that skates and trains."

"So, if I found somewhere in Bridgewater where you could safely skate, and gave you a few nights of work at the club's bar, you'd be able to live with me?"

My heart ached at the hope in his voice. It wasn't that I didn't want to be with Nitro as much as possible, I did. But I didn't want to be one of those girls who lost the rest of her life when she settled on a man. He was being supportive of my roller derby commitment, which was good, but I didn't want to lose my friends at Titanium either. Although, the drive between Bridgewater and Houston wouldn't be so bad if it was only a few nights a week.

"Would you let me still work at least a night or two per week at Titanium? I'd miss my friends there if I left completely."

"I don't see why you couldn't. But I'd like to see this place before I go agreeing to anything to do with it. What about Retro Funk? Would you want to keep working there?"

My stomach clenched as I thought about not working there anymore.

"That shop was my Grandma's pride and joy. I loved working in there with her and had hoped to keep running the store after she passed. But that didn't happen. Mom told me that Grandma wanted me to live my life with no pressure from her to continue her dreams. So Aunt Skye took the store. And my aunt is a grade-A bitch. She resents the hell out of me and the fact she has to keep me employed there as long as I want to be. Honestly? I don't love it like I used to. And I get the feeling Aunt Skye wants to overhaul the store and sell different stuff. Higher end clothing and that kind of thing. Grandma was a hippy to her very soul, but somehow that gene skipped right over Aunt Skye. The high end stuff will be much more to her taste and style. But she can't do that while I'm still working there. I'm not sure of all the legalities, but from my aunt's rants, it was part of the agreement of her getting the store that as long as I was there, she had to keep it as it is. So, yeah, I'll be sad to leave it, but I've known for a while now that I was going to have to go soon."

"If you wanted, you could open your own store in Bridgewater. I've probably got enough cash stashed away for you to make a go of it."

Tears pricked my eyes and tracked down my cheeks as my heart burst with happiness. I wrapped my arms around his neck and feathered kisses over his face. I couldn't believe he'd do that for me. Spend his life savings so I could have my own store! Even if it never happened, the fact he'd even thought of doing it was enough.

He was chuckling by the time I pulled back to look him in the eye, but before I could speak, to tell him how wonderful he was, my phone dinged with a new message and wiping my tears aside, I unlocked the screen.

"Natalie says you're fine to come along tonight. She'll get you to fill out the paperwork while I'm setting up."

"Excellent. Can't wait to see what this place is all about."

Taking his now empty coffee mug, I set it on the table along with my phone, then straddling his lap, I cupped his face in my palms and proceeded to kiss the hell out of my man. Hoping with everything in me that he would like what he saw tonight, that he would be willing to try out at least some of it with me. I started squirming on his lap as I imagined what it would be like to be tied up by him.

Chapter 7

Nitro

After Cindy's explanation earlier today, I was a little worried about what I was going to find at Titanium. Especially after she told me she wanted to keep working there so she could see her friends even if she did move back to Bridgewater. On the plus side, she'd seemed okay with the idea of moving in with me—at least she hadn't flatly refused and told me to fuck off. I was calling that a win.

Since Cin seemed as nervous as I was about tonight, I'd suggested she drive us there in her car, leaving my bike safely in her apartment building's parking garage. She'd been more than happy to drive, and got us there in record time. From the outside it didn't look like much, but obviously it was a private club that you wouldn't be able to find by just wandering down the street. Before I could get too good a look at the exterior, Cin was grabbing my hand and dragging me over toward the door. After passing a badge over a security panel, the large metal door swung open and I found myself standing in the entrance of a sex club. Sorry, not a sex club, a BDSM club.

I'd met Natalie at the derby practice I'd gone to the night before so I recognized her waiting for us when we came in. She strode over and I was a little taken back at what she was wearing. It was completely different from the leggings and t-shirt she'd worn at derby practice, that's for sure. A red leather corset with a matching mini skirt that laced up either side. She had thigh-high black leather boots on and her long, dark hair was down around her shoulders. She looked like a woman in full control of everything around her. It was a little daunting, even to me, a Charon who was used to commanding respect everywhere I went.

"Nitro, it's wonderful to see you here! I hope you like my club. Maybe you can convince our girl here to leave the bar and play a little. I think every Dom we have has tried at some point over the years but she's shut them all down. Myself included."

"Mistress Natalie, your offer to train me was most generous but I just couldn't bring myself to accept it at the time."

She gently cupped my girl's face in her palm as she smiled at her. "And now I've met your man, I know why."

I wasn't sure what the hell to think, let alone say, so I kept my hand on Cin's waist as I stood there silently.

"Right, well, normally I get newbies to go over all the paperwork here before they're allowed in the club, but since you're here so early and Cindy needs to get changed, then set up, you can come on through to the bar and I'll sit with you there and go over everything. You don't need to change, unless you want to, but you do need to take off your club colors. We don't allow them inside. I can arrange for you to have a locker in the men's change room, or if you want to keep things simpler for tonight, Cindy can put it in her locker?"

"I trust Cin to look after it for me."

I shrugged out of my cut and put it over my girl's shoulders. She slipped her arms through the holes and I didn't miss the way she pressed her nose to the shoulder to inhale against the leather. Thing looked huge on her small frame but fuck, it looked right.

"Excellent. You can head off, Cindy. I'll take care of your man until you get back."

Before she could run off, I grabbed her for a fast kiss and gave her a tap on the ass as she moved away from me. Fuck, she looked good wearing my colors. I definitely needed to check with Scout that he'd ordered her property patch.

"Oh, you'll fit right in here, Nitro. Or do you prefer Johnny? Cindy told me she thought you'd prefer Nitro."

"Nitro is what everyone, except for Cin, calls me."

"Excellent. Nitro it is. Please follow me." She began walking in the direction Cin had gone earlier. "Normally there's a pair of greeters in this first room when you arrive, but as I said, since you're early, things aren't rolling just yet. Part of the greeters' job is to make sure no one gets in who shouldn't. I would hope that whoever it is that is stalking our girl hasn't been able to get into the club."

"Do you run checks on everyone who wants to join?"

"That's just not possible. This is a private club, Nitro. No one would want to join if we ran invasive checks on everyone. Not to mention the cost of such a thing. But that's not to say we let just anyone in. Most new members are people like yourself, a partner of a current member. Also, we get friends and sometimes family of members who want to join." She smirked at me. "That one can be fun on the floor when someone is trying to avoid seeing the bare ass of their sibling who's a shameless exhibitionist." She chuckled like she was remembering that very thing happening. Made me glad to be an only child. "Back to your question—every new member has to have a current member nominate them. It's the only way in."

"So, that type of system would make it hard for Cin's stalker to find a way around it?"

We arrived at another door but she didn't move to go through it yet.

"Oh, they could if they wanted to. But it would take some planning. First, he'd have to work out we're a BDSM club, then he'd need to learn at least a little about the basics. He would then have to seduce one of our sweet little subbies until they brought him in with them. So, it could happen. I doubt it has, but Cindy is right to still play things safe even when she's in here. The fact she hasn't received anything from her stalker about working here has me thinking he doesn't know what this place even is. If he, or she, is that possessive of her that they don't even like her talking to other men, I can't see them being happy with her working at a club like mine."

"Cin thinks her stalker is a male, you don't?"

Natalie gave me a broad smile that, to be honest, was more than a touch scary. "I've been here at Titanium for a long time and I've seen just about every type of love, lust and obsession there is. Women can love just as fiercely and possessively as men do. Honestly? Cindy's stalker most likely is male, but it could be a woman. I can tell you she's had just as many female Dommes drool over her here as male Doms.

"Now, through this door is the main floor of Titanium. There's several smaller themed rooms, along with a series of privacy rooms. But this main area is where most of the action takes place, and this is where Cin stays. The main floor is broken up into two areas, the first is the bar area where people sit and mingle until they decide to go play. There's a drink limit, of course. For each alcoholic drink people get a stamp on their hand. After one, they can't do any hardcore scenes, after three, they can't play at all."

"And how in the hell do you monitor that?"

She cocked her brow at my outburst and I cleared my throat before mumbling a quick apology.

"We have Dungeon Monitors who keep an eye on all the scenes that are being run. And if Cindy happens to see someone she knows has three stamps wander into the scening area, she'll alert one of the monitors to the situation."

We were through the door and halfway across the bar area when I stopped short.

What the fuck?

Natalie chuckled. "I gather you've never been into a club like mine before, Nitro?"

"That would be a hell no. And Cin didn't explain this nearly well enough."

A little more warning would have been nice. And I would have greatly preferred Cin here with me right now rather than Natalie. Just glancing at the large crosses on the walls, and the benches and tables, all of which had some type of cuffs or shackles hanging from them had me mentally putting Cin on them. Bound and helpless while I buried myself deep inside her body over and over. Fuck, could Natalie see my hard-on? It was a little dim in here. Hopefully she'd missed it.

"Come and have a seat, I'll give you a little crash course in BDSM."

With my interest piqued, I followed the woman and sat in the seat next to her.

"Now, to start with, I want to make it clear that everything that happens here is consensual and safe. The Doms are monitored closely, and the subs all have a safeword. They say the word 'red' and the scene stops and a DM, Dungeon Monitor, takes them back to a privacy room where they can sort out what happened in private. Most of the time the DM leaves the Dom to take care of the sub, but there's been a time or two where a sub has requested otherwise."

"Natalie, I'm sorry, but I only understood about half of what you just said."

She gave me a gentle smile, like one you'd give to a toddler you were trying to teach. It grated on my nerves but I held myself together. This shit was apparently important to my girl, so I needed to at least try to understand it. And it was also more than just spanking her ass and tying her up, which was where my brain had gone the moment I saw all those crosses and shit.

"Please, call me Mistress Natalie inside the club. Okay, let's start with the basics. BDSM is all about dominance and submission. It can be between two, three or any number of people, but for my explanation, I'll use a male/female couple as an example. One person is the dominant and the other is the submissive, or one is the top while the other is the bottom. The difference between those two is whether there is a power exchange in the mix. You see, a submissive chooses to give their power over to their Dom, they submit to them and the Dom takes and cherishes that gift offered to them. Power is exchanged between the two. With a Top/bottom, it's more about sensation. There's no prior agreement to exchange power between them. You'll see plenty of examples once our guests start coming in and scening. And you can always come find me to ask questions if you have them later." She paused and pointed a finger toward me. "And no thinking that it's always the male that is the dominant or top, although we do have a number of male Doms here, we also have plenty of female Dommes, like myself. The Dom or Top isn't always the physically stronger of the pair. A sub submits to their Dom because they choose to, not because they are forced to. I've Dommed a number of men who would have easily been able to overpower me, but because they chose to submit, to give me that power over them, they didn't even try to. My club is open to all, Doms, subs, Tops, bottoms, switches... my door is open to everyone. Does that all make sense?"

"Switches?"

"Switches are people who switch between being a Dom or a sub, or a Top or a bottom, depending on who they're playing with, but I won't confuse you with that one tonight."

Cindy came through the doorway and after a concerned glance in my direction, headed behind the bar to start the process of getting everything set up for the night.

"Cin is definitely a submissive. And now she's confided to me about her stalker, I can see all that she'd gone through on her own. Well, I can see why she would want this type of relationship with her man. And I've seen it in her gaze many times over the years. She craves having a Dom to take care of her. For so long she's been forced to take control of everything in her world, to be so very careful of every step she takes, of who she talks to.

A good Dom would be able to give her a break from that, a place where she could let go of all her fears and worries and just be in the moment."

"I hope you're not suggesting I should back off for some other man to step in and take care of my girl?"

I was trying my best to not curse up a storm but I was getting close to completely losing my shit at this woman.

"Oh, of course not! I'm implying that *you* be that Dom for her. If you want, I'd be happy to give you some pointers. We also have training sessions each week on a Sunday afternoon." She put down the clipboard she'd been carrying on the table in front of her. "I really think it's something Cin could benefit from. I don't know you well enough yet to say, but from what I know about bikers in general, I think you'll find your place here quite easily too. Please fill out this form at some point tonight, and feel free to watch any of the scenes you'd like to, but I ask that you watch from here in the bar area this evening. If you like what you see and want to have a go, I'll arrange to set something up for you at training this Sunday."

"Thanks. I think. Can I sit at the bar and do this?"

With a chuckle she gave a nod before she stood and moved away. Standing myself, I snatched up the clipboard and headed over to where Cin was finishing off getting set up. It wasn't until I got closer that I could see well enough to notice what she was wearing. I leaned over the bar to get a better look at her lower half.

"Fuck, Cin."

She paused and glanced over her shoulder at me with a smirk.

"What? Don't you like it?"

My girl wasn't dressed like a pin-up tonight. Nope. She was still wearing a pair of her sexy as fuck stockings with a garter belt, but now they were teamed up with a skin-tight black skirt that was so short, it revealed the lacy tops of those stockings. Her shirt was made of a fine mesh that showed her black bra beneath, over the top of the shirt she wore a harness type thing that had straps going all different directions in a way that made her tits stand out like they were spot lit.

"I like it just fine, I'm just not sure about how many men I'm gonna have to kill by the end of the night for drooling over what's mine."

"And women."

That had my head jerking up. After the info dump Natalie just unloaded, I wasn't sure I could handle too much sass from Cin on top of it. "What the fuck do you mean?"

She laughed and set a beer down in front of me.

"Didn't Mistress Natalie tell you? Everyone is welcome here, babe. Gay, straight, bi, trans… so it's not just the men who'll be drooling. But don't worry too much. While anyone can look, they all know better than to even attempt to touch me. Mistress Natalie runs a tight ship—she doesn't tolerate any bullshit, and won't stand for anyone trying to get rough with her staff. She's an awesome boss."

I didn't respond as I recalled what Cin and Natalie had said out in the entrance, about Natalie training Cin. I took a large mouthful of beer as I tried to push aside the image of the two women together. I knew it hadn't happened, but damn, every man on the planet had at least a few girl-on-girl fantasies. And I just got a new one.

Cindy

I tried not to laugh as Nitro drained his beer in a couple of swallows. Poor man really hadn't known anything about the lifestyle. I wasn't sure how that could be. I'd been certain since those Fifty Shades movies had come out, everyone knew at least a little, but apparently not MC members. Grabbing the stamp, I leaned over and pressed it against the back of his hand twice before I set his next drink down. Marking another drink down against my account.

"I know you're not scening tonight, but I always follow the rules."

He tapped the tip of the pen against the form as a smirk grew across his face.

"Is that right? And what would happen if you broke the rules?"

Was he screwing around or serious? I chewed on my lower lip as I tried to work out how to respond.

"Would Mistress Natalie spank you for it?"

I rolled my eyes. Yep, he was screwing around.

"I bet you'd just love to watch me strapped down to a spanking bench with Mistress Natalie spanking my bare ass while you watched. Pervert."

"Oh, now there's a scene I could get behind. Literally. And of course he is, you need a good pervert, pet."

My cheeks flared hot with embarrassment as Natalie came up beside me and gave me a little hip check before she grabbed a bottle of water from the fridge and marked it against her account.

"Nitro, you let me know if you want me to act that one out for you. I'd be happy to oblige. Added bonus for me would be that I'd be the envy of every Dom here for being the first to leave my mark on the most unattainable sub we've ever had here."

With a wink, she sauntered off and I let silence fill the space for a minute before I worked up the nerve to glance at his face. His focus was solely on me and I could clearly see the lust in his gaze.

"I'm thinking I might like this place, Cin, but I'll be the first one to leave a mark on you. Not her."

Pulling my own bottle of water out, I took a large gulp as I watched Nitro get busy filling out the form that would make him a member.

What the fuck had just happened? I mean I'd hoped Nitro would react favorably to Titanium, but this was beyond that. And was he seriously implying he'd let me scene with Natalie? I wasn't sure how I felt about that one. I wasn't bi, I'd never been sexually attracted to a woman in my life, but the thought of Nitro watching me bottom for Natalie before he took me back to a privacy room definitely had my interest piqued.

I took another deep drink of water and tried to clear my thoughts as the first few people started coming into the club. It was time to work, and fight off gossip. I knew me having a man with me would be big news and would spread like wildfire. Over the twelve years I'd been working here, I'd had many a Dom try to woo me out from behind the bar. It helped that Natalie had publicly made me off limits a long time ago, but it didn't change the way people spoke about me. Apparently it was strange that I had stayed single for so long.

The chances of my stalker getting access inside Titanium were slim, I knew that. It was why I'd initially loved working here so much. I didn't have to watch over my shoulder the entire time. Then I made friends with so many of the regulars and I loved working here even more. Didn't hurt that Natalie let me eat for free on the nights or days I worked. She had a chef on staff so people could order meals before or after they played, which a lot of people took advantage of. But none of that changed the fact that if I had decided to risk it and start playing with a Dom, at some point they would have wanted to meet outside the club and that I couldn't have ever risked. Well, and if I'm going to be honest with myself, nor could any of the men here compete with the memory of Johnny. I mean Nitro. I was grateful he didn't seem to mind me calling him Johnny when it was just the two of us, but I was trying really hard to remember to call him Nitro when we were out.

There might have been only a handful of people in the bar area when Natalie came over to take Nitro's completed form, but every one of them watched the interaction. A new member always got attention, but as soon as they realized he was here with me, things would really heat up for us both.

Trew, an unattached subbie, came up to the other end of the bar and I steeled myself for the first round of questions. Trew was a sweetheart, but one of the worst gossips Titanium had.

"Hey, Trew, what can I get you?"

"Details about our newest acquisition. He has that Dom feel to him. What's his name? Does he have a sub? Is he gay, straight or bi?"

I laughed. I couldn't help it. Trew threw out questions so fast, there was no way I could have answered any of them. And since he was bi, and adored big, strong, alpha male Doms, I'd known Nitro would have his attention the moment Trew saw him.

"Slow your roll. His name is Nitro, and sorry to disappoint you but he's straight."

He frowned at me. "Are you sure? Because—"

I held up my palm to stop him. "I'm quite sure, because he's with me."

For at least a full minute, Trew stood there blinking at me like I'd set off a bomb or something.

"Get. Out. You found yourself a Dom? A hunky one at that. At last!"

He held his palm up high so I gave in and gave him a high-five.

"Well, he's not technically a Dom, at least not yet. Although, it looks like he's keen on learning."

That had Trew's eyes gleaming. "You found yourself a vanilla boy to corrupt? Such fun. So, are you the top, bottom or are you going to switch it up?" He dramatically wriggled his eyebrows. "You know, none of us have ever been able to work it out for sure. Most think you're a subbie."

The very thought of trying to top Nitro had me laughing so hard my eyes teared up.

"Oh, honey, there is no way that man would take to me trying to top him. Although, it might be fun to try on occasion. He's always been one-hundred-percent alpha male, that one."

"That sounds like you've got some history. Is he the reason you've been the club's resident spinster all these years?"

I rolled my eyes as Simoni slipped in next to Trew and joined the conversation. Clearly her Dom, Dilan, had given her permission to come and get the news.

"You two are terrible, you know? Yes, there's history. We dated back in high school, then we ran into each other in Austin after the last derby match we went to over there."

Simoni's expression lit up. "Oh, I want to know what happened that you lost contact for so long. Please tell us!"

I pulled out two bottles of water. "Not right now, guys. I gotta get working. Water, or something stronger tonight?"

Both their expressions dropped like I'd just offered them sour milk to drink but they accepted their water bottles and headed off from the bar, letting me serve others, and repeat the information about Nitro. I had a feeling I was going get tired of saying the same thing over and over. Maybe I should have made a sign to hang around my neck, explaining things.

Chapter 8

Nitro

My evening at Titanium had been eye opening to say the least. The scenes I saw, even from a distance, were intense. Floggings, whippings, bondage, role playing… that place had it all going on. The first time I saw, and heard, the crack of a whip I tensed, worried for the woman being whipped, but Natalie had been close by and obviously watching for my reaction. She took me closer to the scene so I could see the girl's face and hear her Dom check with her if she was okay. Her breathy voice as she said she was green, had me relaxing. Natalie had sat with me again later and explained how there was not only a safeword that would stop everything—red—but two more. Yellow meant the scene would get paused and reassessed before continuing, and green meant go, that everything was fine.

I was extremely grateful for all the time Natalie spent with me explaining various things, and introducing me to a few of the Doms. I could easily see myself being friends with a number of them. Most I'd spoken to weren't all that different than my Charon brothers. They liked to be in control and to take care of those they loved. They also liked to play some games in the bedroom, and out of it. I was glad Cin had found this place, and the people within it. Everyone I talked to spoke highly of Cin and many mentioned they'd been worried about her over the years as she never came out from behind the bar to play or live a little. I hated my girl had spent so many years alone, but I was also grateful that it meant she was single now so I could make her mine again. And I vowed that she would never find herself alone again.

With a sigh, I glanced over at the clock on her bedside table. I needed to get moving. After we left the club, we'd come back to her place and we'd both been so damn horny, we'd barely made it inside her room before I had her naked and pressed up against the wall. But now it was morning, and I had to head back to Bridgewater for the day. I couldn't miss church, and I needed to catch up on some paperwork and ordering for Styxx. The others could keep it going without me, but ordering stock and finalizing the payroll so Arrow, the club's treasurer, could pay everyone, still fell to me.

Cin looked so fucking sweet as she slept. I hated to have to wake her, especially when it wasn't to take her again. But I needed to head out and had already left it about as late as I could. Lifting my hand, I gently rubbed the backs of my knuckles over her cheek.

"Hey, babe, wake up."

With a moan she rubbed her cheek against my hand, but didn't open her eyes. I chuckled and leaned in to press a kiss to her lips, not stopping until she'd opened up beneath me and started kissing me back. I pulled back from her lips and she wriggled over closer to me, trying to get more attention.

"Needy little thing, aren't you?" I stroked the hair out of her face. "I wish I could stay, I really do, but I gotta head out today. I need to go take care of some stuff back home."

That had her opening her eyes and blinking up at me, shock clear in her gaze. I frowned down at her, and locked my arm around her to prevent her from getting away from me when she started to shuffle back.

"What the fuck, Cin? I have to go for one day and you're kicking me to the curb?"

"You made it sound like you were done with me."

I thought back over what I'd said, but couldn't figure out how the fuck I'd given her that impression.

"Babe, let's get this straight right now. I ain't ever gonna be done with you. I just need to head back to Bridgewater for the day. We have church and I have to deal with paperwork and ordering supplies for Styxx, the club's bar. Hopefully I'll be back here with you by tonight."

She ran a hand over my chest, her fingers sifting through the hair there for a moment before she spoke.

"You want to come to Titanium with me again tonight?"

"Sure, I enjoyed last night. I know I'll be hanging out at the bar again, but that's okay. It'll give me a chance to chat to some of the Doms again."

She smiled up at me. "Can't tell you how happy it makes me that you're being so accepting. I might not have scened yet, but after spending so many years being surrounded by it, it's something I've always wanted to try."

With a smile, I leaned in and pressed a kiss to her forehead. "I picked up on that, babe. And honestly, I really liked the few I met last night. They remind me of my club brothers in a lot of ways. I can see myself fitting in easily there—with you by my side, of course."

She chuckled. "You mean with me at your feet."

"That's going to take some getting used to. Not sure I like the idea of you on your knees." She cut me off with a loud bark of laughter, and I joined her when I realized what I'd said. "Not like that, babe. I'll always like you on your knees if you've got my dick in your mouth."

"I knew what you meant, but I couldn't help but laugh. So, how soon do you need to get going?"

As she spoke her hand crept down and wrapped around my erection, making me groan as she stroked me. I glanced at the clock and figured, what the fuck, I was already going to be late, I might as well enjoy it and make the lecture I'd get worth it.

"Join me in the shower, babe."

The grin that spread over her face, and the way her eyes lit with mischief was a look I'd never tire of seeing.

She released her hold on me as I rolled over, then after I stood, I turned back, scooping her off the mattress before tossing her gently over my shoulder, and giving her ass a slap once she was settled, earning me a squeal.

"Yeah, I think I really like this whole Dom caveman thing."

She laughed as I strode toward her bathroom. I flipped the tap on before I let her slide down my front until her feet were on the floor. She turned to face the water, and I let her deal with adjusting the flow as I ran my palms over her curves. With a moan, she arched her back before taking a step under the water. I followed her but before I could grab her again, she'd turned to face me, gripped my hips in her palms and started lowering herself down to her knees.

My cock jerked, hard, at the sight of her like that.

"Okay, yeah, I fucking love how you look on your knees, babe. Especially when you've got your mouth full. Open up, Cin."

She dutifully opened her mouth and after wrapping my fist around my cock, I lined the tip up with her lips and slipped just the head inside.

"Run your tongue over me, oh yeah, fuck. Just. Like. That."

Her tongue was warm and soft as it stroked over the head of my dick. She lapped at the slit, humming as she got a taste of my pre cum.

"Take the rest of me in, babe. Breathe through your nose and take as much as you can."

She leaned in and took half my length before she pulled back, licking the tip before she had another go at swallowing me. Fuck, I'd never seen anything as sexy as my girl on her knees, water dripping from her hair as she did her best to take my entire length. On the fourth pass, she got nearly all the way there, but I could tell she was struggling and since we didn't have a heap of time, I pulled free and pulled her up to her feet.

Before she could say a word I took her mouth and kissed the hell out of her. Without breaking the kiss, I lifted one of her legs over my hip and thrust deep inside her. She moaned into my mouth as her nails dug into my shoulders. Her tight, hot channel clenched against my cock when I broke the kiss and tweaked her nipples. With her back pressed up against the tile, and the water pounding against my spine, I let loose and fucked her hard and fast, holding her gaze with mine the entire time.

It didn't take long for my balls to tighten up, not after watching her on her fucking knees earlier. I slipped my hand between us, rubbing my thumb over her clit until she was trembling with the need to come. But she held it off, dragging the moment out, and I felt my control slipping.

"C'mon, babe. Let it go and take me with you."

No way was I coming before she did. Thankfully, my words seem to be what she needed, and calling out my name, she bucked against me as her pussy gripped my cock, holding me in as I started to come. Filling her up.

Ah, fuck. I hadn't gloved up. I knew I should pull out, but there was no way in hell I could stop this train now it had started. Thrusting up deep inside her, I filled her womb with my seed. Part of me hoped like fuck it did its job and tied her to me forever, and the other part wanting more time with her before we added a kid to the mix.

As soon as I could, I pulled free of her and grabbed the soap, washing her from head to toe, before quickly washing myself down. Flipping off the water, I followed her out of the stall. She handed me a towel, still silent. I wrapped it around my waist before grabbing the other one to begin drying her off.

"Cindy, I'm so fucking sorry. I didn't even think of grabbing a condom. I shouldn't have taken you bare like that, without discussing it with you first. I'm so sorry."

I froze when her palms came up and cupped my face. "Johnny, don't ever regret being with me. Neither of us are exactly teenagers, if I get pregnant we'll deal with it."

"Are you serious right now?"

I wasn't sure how to take what she'd just said.

"Johnny, I'm thirty-five years old, and you're two years older than me. Time is slipping past us to have kids. One of the things that has always cut me the deepest is that this stalker has prevented me from having the family I'd always dreamed of having. And there's no one I'd rather have a baby with than you."

Fuck it all, but my eyes started stinging. So she wouldn't notice, I took her mouth with mine and kissed her until I felt more in control of my emotions. This woman was one in a million, no doubt about it.

"Woman, you slay me. You truly do, and I hate that I have to leave, but Scout's gonna have my hide for being late to church as it is."

Cindy

He tried to distract me with his kiss, but I saw the sheen of tears in his eyes. He claimed I was the one who slayed him, but I think it was the other way around. He absolutely slayed me. But I didn't want to get any deeper in our conversation right now, not when he had to run out the door.

"Church? You get today's Thursday, not Sunday, right?"

I followed him as, laughing, he moved back into my bedroom where we both made quick work of getting dressed.

"Not that kinda church, babe. Church is what we call our meetings. No idea why, it's just how it is. What are your plans today?"

"I've got some laundry to do this morning, then I'm at Retro Funk this afternoon. After that is derby practice, then on to Titanium."

He shook his head. "You're so damn busy all the time. Can you text the boys what times you're gonna be where? So they know when to watch for you being on the move."

I shrugged and pulled out my phone, Nitro had put in Keg's and Jazz's numbers for me last week. "Sure, I've been doing that most days anyhow. And as far as being busy, I didn't have anything else to do, and honestly? I didn't want the spare time where I'd be forced to what? Sit around thinking about everything I didn't have but wanted. It was easier to stay busy. I'll work on cutting back now that I have you in my life, promise."

He gave me a heart-stopping smile before he kissed me again, turning me into a pile of goo before he pulled back and declared he really had to leave this time. Thankfully, before he made it out the door, enough of my brain cells were firing that I remembered what I needed to give him.

"Let me grab the spare gate opener for you before you go, or you won't make it out of the garage."

Once he had the opener, he was jogging out the door and I was left to try to process all that had happened in the last couple of days. After locking the door, I made my way back to my bedroom, which still smelled of Johnny and sex. I'd certainly broken my dry spell with a bang and a half.

I made quick work of stripping the sheets from the bed and grabbing the towels from the bathroom before tossing them all in the basket with my clothes. Since I was spending my morning at home, I'd dressed for comfort in a pair of leggings and a loose fitting hoodie.

After I slipped my phone and keys into the hoodie's pocket, I grabbed my basket and headed out the door. One of the downsides to this apartment building was that the laundry was a separate room down on the ground floor. The upside was, since nearly everyone who lived in the building worked during the day, I had the room to myself most weeks. That meant I could use all the washers at the same time, making the process so much faster than if I had to wait around for just one machine to do everything.

As I started to put the sheets into a machine, I began to attempt to come to terms with the fact that I'd had unprotected sex with Nitro while I wasn't on any birth control. I'd played it cool in front of him, of course, but inside I was panicking. My life wasn't ready for a baby. What would my stalker do if he discovered I was pregnant? Would he attempt to hurt my unborn baby somehow? Would that be what finally pushed him to the point of hurting me?

As I was lost in thought, I automatically went through my Thursday routine, and before I knew it, I had a basket full of clean laundry and was on my way back to the apartment, still with no real clue what to think about the fact I was potentially pregnant. I'd just opened the door when my phone rang. Dropping the basket onto the floor, I pulled out my mobile and seeing it was Aunt Skye, I wondered what could be wrong, so quickly answered to find out.

"Hey Aunt Skye, what's up?"

I hoped she wasn't calling to say she didn't need me in the shop today. She didn't do that often, thankfully, but when she did, she always refused to pay me for the time and I had to rework my budget for the next couple of weeks around the loss. Not that my aunt gave a shit about that.

"Oh, Cindy, it's horrible! Someone set fire to the shop last night!"

Shock had me silent for a couple minutes. I couldn't have heard her right.

"Cindy? Are you still there?"

"Ah, yeah, I'm here. Sorry, what did you say happened?"

I also wanted to ask why she'd waited until now to call me with the news of something that had happened last night. If she hadn't found out last night, she would have known first thing this morning. Since it was currently late morning, I knew she'd known for hours at least, and not bothered to tell me.

"The police said the firefighters think it was a Molotov cocktail that was thrown through the front window. I can't imagine who would do such a thing. Maybe they'll be wrong and it turns out to be faulty wiring or something."

My gut clenched and roiled. I knew exactly who would do it. I also knew it had nothing to do with freaking faulty wiring. My stalker was backed into a corner, unable to get near me, so he'd lashed out at the shop. But I couldn't tell Aunt Skye that.

"I have no idea, are you at the shop now? I'll come straight over."

"What? Oh, no you don't need to head over. There's not much to be done. You just say home for the day. Maybe go out with that young man who's been following you around."

I grit my teeth and counted to ten quickly before I responded. Everyone in the family knew how I felt about that shop, knew I'd want to see the damage first hand to see if it was going to be salvageable. I also knew she didn't give a shit about my dating life.

"I want to be there. I'll see you soon."

"But—"

Before she could argue any more, I hung up and, after picking up my basket, rushed for my room. I didn't bother changing, just tossed the laundry on my bed and grabbed my handbag before heading back out the door.

I was starting my car before I remembered my bodyguards, I'd given them my schedule earlier and it obviously didn't include my current outing. I pulled my phone out again and shot a text off to Keg, Jazz and Nitro, letting them know where I was heading and why, then I shifted my focus solely onto getting to the shop as fast as I could.

When I pulled into the parking lot, it was nearly empty, which was strange for this time of day. But I guessed the fire trucks had been taking up the space earlier. The rear of the shop didn't look too bad. The back door was missing and there were some black soot marks up the wall above the empty doorway. But I knew the inside would look a lot worse. This row of shops was old and had been built from solid stone. A fire would have to be extremely hot to damage the exterior walls. There was also water everywhere, puddles on the ground, and the air had a bite to it, smelling of smoke and a horrible mix of everything that had been burned inside the shop. The police had put tape up across the doorway but I couldn't see anyone around.

"Aunt Skye?"

After locking my car, I rushed up to the doorway, scanning the area for my aunt or anyone else, as I took in the destruction in front of me. After several minutes, I still hadn't seen anyone, but the level of damage was clear. I doubted anything much was going to be salvageable. Emotion clogged my throat and I battled against the urge to drop to the ground and cry. I barely noticed the roar of the Harleys until they were pulling up behind me, their engines now so loud my body vibrated with it. I turned to see who it was, because it sounded like more than just the one bike I'd normally had following me around. It was only when I started to turn that I noticed that Keg was at the end of the block of shops and looked like he'd been there for a while. I returned his head tilt with a grim smile before moving to look at the new arrivals. Naturally, Nitro's big, golden yellow bike was at the front, and there were three others behind it. All four of the men were wearing leather cuts that declared they were members of the Charon MC.

The moment they all killed their engines, the air around us seemed to still. I didn't know what to say or do, I felt shattered inside. So much of Grandma was in this place. And now it was gone. And what did I say to a man who'd obviously received my message and came straight back to me. I doubted he even got a full hour in Bridgewater before he turned and came back. I knew he wasn't making shit up this morning, he really must have work to do back in Bridgewater. He'd spent so much time with me over the past week, he had to be falling behind with whatever he normally did with his days.

I stayed frozen to the spot as he lifted his leg and swung off his ride. His every movement was smooth and sexy as hell. Even in my shocked, devastated state, I couldn't fail to notice and appreciate his masculinity. In seconds he was standing in front of me and pulling me in against him. The moment his strong arms surrounded me, the tears started. All my emotions bubbled up and I clung to him as I let myself fall apart. This place held so many memories, working with my Grandma, seeing her help customers, even if it was just chatting to them. She wasn't so focused on sales like my aunt was. Grandma was more interested in helping people. More than once, she'd given clothing to someone in need, or taken them down the street to buy them lunch.

But she'd been gone for twelve years, and now her shop, her legacy, was gone too. And it was all my fault. If I'd just resisted Nitro, my stalker wouldn't have upped the stakes like this!

"C'mon, Cin. You're gonna make yourself sick."

I tried to push him away but he only loosened his hold, he didn't let go completely.

"We can't be together. Not if this is what is going to happen. I can't lose anything else to him."

His expression hardened and his grip shifted to hold my shoulders.

"If you really mean that, then you're letting him take this away from us, too. You say you can't lose anything else, but in the same sentence throw me away because of him. Do I mean so little to you?"

More tears rolled down my cheeks as I trembled in his grip. He was right, I knew he was. But I didn't know what else I could do, how to stop this nut-job.

"I don't want to see you hurt."

Chapter 9

Nitro

I knew she was lashing out with the first idea that came to her because she was overwhelmed and hurting, but there was no way in hell I was going to let her push me aside to appease this fucker. Not ever again.

"I don't want to see you hurt."

I shifted my grip so I was holding her neck in one palm and her cheek in the other.

"Babe, you kicking me out of your life will hurt me. And I hope this fucker does try to come after me, because, babe, it'll be last thing he ever does. And then you'll be free of him."

That had her freezing for a moment before she relaxed a little and her gaze softened. I pressed a short kiss to her lips before moving my arms to hold her tightly against me again.

"Did you get another note yet? You know this might be a random act. Your aunt's not exactly the nicest person in the world, babe."

"When she called, she tried to sound like she'd only just found out, but look at it. This was all over hours ago and she's not even here."

I took that as a no on the note front. The hurt in her tone tore at me. She loved this place, and for her aunt to not call her the moment she'd known would be tearing her up almost as much as the damage from the actual fire.

"Why don't we drop your car back at your place, and you come for a ride with me back to Bridgewater? I'll show you around the clubhouse and Styxx. You can meet some of the men and their old ladies, might even be able to find a baby or two for you to cuddle."

I knew if I really wanted her to seriously consider moving to Bridgewater to live with me, I had to make her fall in love with the place. Hopefully, if she met a few of the other old ladies, and their babies, along with more of my brothers, she'd feel more comfortable with the idea. And c'mon, what woman didn't get cheered up by babies? Her body lifted a little as she took a deep breath and I dropped my arms away as she pressed against me so she could stand on her own.

"Well, it's not like I've got anything else to do until tonight now. It might be nice to get out of Houston for the day. Um, who's with you?"

I winced as I realized I'd completely ignored my brothers from the moment we'd pulled up.

"Ah, fuck. Sorry, completely forgot to do introductions." I paused as she wiped at her face and took a few deep breaths, then with my palms on her shoulders, turned until we both faced my brothers who were all still sitting on their bikes waiting for me to indicate what the fuck we were going to do next.

"Men, this is my girl Cindy. Cindy, this is Mac, Arrow and Keys. Three of my Charon MC brothers."

"Hi. Ah, sorry I interrupted whatever it was ya'll were doing earlier."

All three got off their bikes and came over to shake her hand. It was Keys who spoke up.

"No worries, sugar. It was just some paperwork. We were all happy to leave that behind and head out for a ride."

That got a small smile out of Cin, but not for long.

"Well, I guess we'll all head back to my apartment, then."

I grabbed her for another kiss before she could climb back into her vehicle. "Are you sure you're okay to drive? I can drive you home then get a ride back with one of the boys to get my bike."

Riding bitch behind any of my brothers would be a moment I'd never live down, but I'd do it for Cin.

She reached up and cupped my cheek in her palm. "You are too sweet. I'm fine to drive. A little heartbreak isn't going to keep me from living my life, Nitro."

I much preferred how she sounded saying Johnny, but I couldn't complain. Not when I had insisted she call me Nitro when we were around other people.

"Okay, we'll be following you. See you in a bit, babe."

With a peck to her cheek, I held her car door open as she climbed in. Once I'd closed her in, I headed back to my bike.

"Follow her down into the garage. After we park, I'll run up with her, then we can all head back to Bridgewater."

"Sounds good, brother."

Slipping back on my bike, I started it up and once Cin drove past, followed her out with my boys at my back. She didn't live far away and within ten minutes we were all pulling up in her apartment building's garage.

"Right, we'll be back down soon."

Leaving my brothers to chill in the garage, I ushered Cin toward the elevator. Now that she'd agreed to spend the day with me, I was anxious to get moving with it. I hadn't managed to get her on the back of my bike yet and the hour or so it was going to take to get from Houston to Bridgewater was going to feel like heaven with her pressed up against my back the whole way.

Once the elevator doors closed and she jabbed the button for the lobby, I wrapped my arm around her waist and held her to me.

"What do I need to wear to ride on your bike?"

That had me grinning. She wasn't thinking about the fire anymore, but about being wrapped around me, on my bike. Before I could answer, the doors opened again and I followed her as she walked over to the mailboxes.

"Jeans, vest or jacket. Have you got some sturdy boots?"

As she slid the key in the box, she smirked over her shoulder at me. "I think I have something that'll work."

I mulled over her words as she gathered the few envelopes that were in the box and then locked things back up again. She didn't look at them as we went back to the elevator.

"What do you mean by that?"

"You'll see."

She began flipping through the envelopes but stopped suddenly. Her face went pale and her breath hitched as she seemed to be suddenly intently focused on whatever it was she held.

"Cin? What is it?"

After a ding, the doors slid open and when Cin still didn't move, I scooped her up and strode down toward her apartment. When we reached her door, she cleared her throat.

"Put me down, please."

Her voice was barely above a whisper. I set her back on her feet and she carefully opened her door. By the time I followed her in, I was worried enough I shot off a text to the boys downstairs to come up. This wasn't going to be a quick stop and go.

Trailing after Cindy, I waited until we were inside her room before I said anything.

"Cindy? What is it?"

She shook her head as she sat heavily on the side of the mattress.

"I knew it was him."

Walking over to her, I dropped down to my knees in front of her. "You mean your stalker? Did he leave you a note?"

She finally looked up from the paper she still held and into my eyes. The agony I could see in their depths hit me like a sucker punch to the gut.

"Can I see it?"

"Do you have to?"

I cupped her face between my palms, stroking my thumbs over her cheeks, trying to decide how to handle her in this situation. She'd told me she wanted my dominance. On top of what Natalie had told me, I'd been doing some Googling so I had a better idea now what she was asking for. But this wasn't a sexual situation, would she want me to take control outside the bedroom? She looked so completely lost and broken right now, I was willing to try just about anything to put her back together again.

Putting a hard edge to my voice to indicate I wasn't negotiating here, I wanted that letter, and she was going to give it to me, I held her gaze as I spoke.

"I need to know as much about this fucker as I can. The more we know, the easier it'll be to catch him. So, yes, you need to hand that over and let me take care of it. To take care of you."

She closed her eyes and winced, so I leaned in and pressed a kiss to her temple.

"We *will* catch him. And no matter what he says in that note, it won't change how I feel about you. Let me be who you need me to be—to be strong enough to take this from you and deal with it."

Her body relaxed as she seemed to finally understand what I was telling her. I reached for the envelope and letter she was still holding and she allowed me to take them from her just as someone started banging on her front door.

"Go have a shower and get ready for our ride, babe. I'm going to let the boys in and see what we can do about this."

After giving her another quick kiss, I stood and headed out of her bedroom with the note in hand. Twisting the lock, I opened the front door and let my brothers inside.

"What's happened now?"

That was Arrow, direct as always.

"Not entirely sure, but she stopped to grab her mail and when she opened this in the elevator, she shut down. She's only just handed it over so I haven't read it yet."

"It from her stalker?"

"That's what she said."

I lifted the note so my brothers could read it as I did. It was clearly written in a rush, the handwriting rough and entirely in capital letters.

"That's one angry fucker."

I grunted at Keys' observation as I read the words. My own anger built with every new word. Yeah, this fucker was mad as hell, and furious that Cindy was defying him. I hated that this shit had cost my girl her grandma's shop.

"He's escalating, and he's going to keep escalating now that I'm back."

I didn't make it a question. We all knew it was the truth.

Keys took the envelope it came in and examined it. "This wasn't posted but delivered. There's no postmark or stamp on it. When we get back to the clubhouse I'll look at the video feeds and see if I can work out who delivered it. Never know our luck, this might just be the break we've been waiting for. How long till we're ready to roll out?"

I glanced at my watch. "I told her to take a shower. I'll go check how she's doing. But I want to get moving ASAP."

Leaving the letter with Keys, I strode back to Cindy's room. When I didn't see her there, I continued on to the bathroom. She was standing at the vanity, leaning her weight on her hands that were on either side of the bowl, with her head hanging forward. She'd wrapped a towel around her middle and in the steamy room, she looked so defeated. The thought she'd let this fucker win after all this time had my temper flaring, but I pushed it down as I walked up behind her. She didn't need my anger. Gathering her hair in my hands, I moved it to the side before I leaned down and pressed a kiss to the top of her shoulder, then the soft skin of her neck.

"Don't let this beat you, Cin. You're stronger than this bastard."

Cindy

I had no intention of letting this asshole beat me, but losing Retro Funk was a deep wound to my heart and soul that I needed more than a second to be able to process.

"I just needed a few minutes. Trust me, I have no fucking intention of laying down for this bastard."

Turning around, I wrapped my arms around Nitro's neck, letting my fingers run through the shorter hair at the base of his skull. I desperately wanted to change the subject, to not talk about, or even think about the stalker who was so insistent on ruining my life.

"You know, this'll be my first ride on your Harley. That's kind of a big deal for you MC boys, isn't it?"

He frowned at me for a moment before his expression cleared and he smirked down at me with a scoff.

"Yeah, babe. Having my old lady on my bike for the first time is a fucking big deal, and you can't do it wearing a towel."

"Not sure I like the whole 'old lady' thing."

With a laugh, he wrapped his palms under my butt and when he lifted me, I wrapped my legs around his waist before he moved us back into the bedroom and over to my closet.

"Just about every old lady I know didn't like the term to start with. Just like them, you'll get used to it and realize it really isn't a negative title. Quite the opposite."

He'd explained to me before about how it works, how an old lady is the property of her man. Sounded all very old-fashioned to me, and I wasn't completely sold on it. But that was part of what today would be about. I'd get to hang out in Bridgewater for the day with the Charon MC and meet some of the other old ladies. See if it would be possible for me to find my place in Bridgewater.

"Okay, well, if you really don't want me going in a towel, you need to put me down and let me get dressed. Because at this point, it's kinda you holding us all up, babe."

With a shake of his head, he lowered me down until I could put my feet on the carpet. Then when I turned to face my closet, he gave my ass a solid smack. Just hard enough for me to feel through the towel. Even though it didn't really hurt, it was a surprise and I turned to glare over my shoulder at him.

"Oww! What the fuck?"

He was smirking again. "Just giving you want you want, Cin. Don't make me wait long or I'll be back in here and you'll be over my knee for a lot more than one."

With that, he strode out of the room and I was left standing there with my mouth gaping open in shock. What just happened? Did Nitro just go all Dom on my ass?

With a smile, I reached into my closet and pulled out my biker boots. I wore them to Titanium sometimes, but it would be fun to tease Nitro about why I had them. The spanking threat was intriguing, but I didn't want to keep the guys waiting, or wait any longer for my first ride on the back of Nitro's wheels. So I rushed to get my underwear before tugging on a pair of jeans, fitted long sleeve shirt, and a jacket. After grabbing a pair of socks, I took my boots over to the bed and got them on as quickly as I could.

Then, after a quick trip back into the bathroom to dump my towel, brush out my hair and put it in a messy braid, I was grabbing my bag and striding out of my room toward the voices I could hear in the living area.

"We ready to go?"

Silence greeted my question, then I got a couple of low whistles as Nitro prowled over to me looking like he was on the hunt.

"Fuck, Cin."

"What? Don't you like what I'm wearing? Is it not suitable?"

I looked down at myself. My jeans were a pair of fitted ones and they hugged my legs and hips perfectly. I'd gone with a plain, black, long sleeve shirt under my vintage-look green leather jacket. The jacket was biker style, with the front zip off to the side and the collar high around my neck.

"You look fucking amazing. But I had no idea you owned actual riding gear. Who's taken you riding before? Natalie?"

I reached up and ran my nails through his scruff, one of my new favorite things to do.

"I kinda want to string this out because you're getting all jealous and being adorable, but I really want to go for this ride." I paused to lick my lips. "I've never been on a bike before. I wear the boots at Titanium every now and then, and I bought the jacket because I love vintage stuff and fell in love with it when it came into the store last year. But it's not a proper bike jacket with all the extra safety stuff built in."

"What you have on is perfectly fine for being on a bike. Damn, it's gonna be a hard ride."

One of the men snickered. Arrow, I think. "Don't you mean you're going to be hard on the ride?"

I bit my lip to stop from laughing when Nitro turned a dark glare his friend's way.

"Shut the fuck up, Arrow. Let's roll out."

Cool. I had it right. Allowing the excitement of my first ride on a Harley to fill my thoughts, I forgot all about that fucking letter as we made our way back down to the garage. At the bikes, Nitro produced a second helmet from somewhere and secured it on me.

"Let me get on first, then hop up behind me. Put your foot on this peg, and swing your other leg over the back. Once you're on and settled, wrap your arms around my waist to hang on. Okay?"

"Sounds good."

I felt like a little kid on Christmas morning. I wanted to get on and go already! To be so close to Nitro, to feel the engine beneath us. He chuckled a little as he swung his leg over and settled on the seat.

"C'mon, Miss Excitable, get your sexy ass saddled up."

With a little squeal that had all the men laughing, I hopped up and plastered myself against Nitro's back. Feeling cheeky, I slipped my palms up under his shirt so they were resting against his six-pack. The muscles tensed beneath my touch and I grinned like a loon when he started the engine and we all headed out of the garage.

I took a deep breath and smiled as Nitro expertly weaved us in and around traffic until we hit the highway. By the time we rolled into Bridgewater about an hour later, I was addicted. I loved the feel of the bike under me, the wind in my face, Nitro so close. It was perfect. I started to wonder if Nitro would let me have my own ride. Did old ladies do that? Or do they have to stay on the back of their man's bike? I shook the thoughts free as I started to see familiar buildings. I'd ask Nitro later about getting my own bike.

I hadn't returned to Bridgewater at all since I'd left. A lot of the town was the same, just with fresher coats of paint. There were a few newer homes and shops, but it looked like the town hadn't had the growth spurt some other cities had experienced over the past nearly two decades.

We pulled in through the big gates that certainly hadn't changed at all. I suspected, other than an occasional new coat of black paint, they hadn't changed at all since the day they'd been installed. The wrought iron was thick and strong, and had "Charon MC" over the top of the gate in an arch. I'd never really seen the actual clubhouse before, other than briefly as I went past on the road, so I couldn't remember anything about its past appearance.

The building itself wasn't anything special to look at from outside, especially when you got an eyeful of the bikes that were sitting in front of it. There were only a couple, but they were gorgeous, gleaming in the sunshine. They were clearly well looked after machines. Nitro turned in front of them and I was so busy checking them out, I nearly missed him tapping my hand to indicate I needed to hop off. After I was free, he shuffled back so his bike was neatly in the line-up. His golden yellow machine was just as perfect as the others. It made sense that MC members would take care of their rides. But this was more than merely maintaining them, these bikes were clearly their owners' pride and joy.

"You want to come in, or do you just want to stand out here all afternoon?"

There was a heavy dose of humor in Nitro's voice.

"More than ready for the rest of the tour. I was just taking a few moments to relish in the knowledge that I'm just realizing how much I love Harleys."

The other men chuckled at me as they made their way ahead of us through the front door of the clubhouse, which was being guarded by another club member. I gave him a smile when he nodded our way. It had to be the most boring job ever, but he seemed content standing there, keeping guard. I wondered what the fuck he must have done wrong to have landed the job.

Once through the door, it took a moment for my eyes to adjust. It was a gorgeous, sunny Texan day today, so even though the clubhouse was well lit, it was still more dull inside than out. The room had a bar along one side, with the rest of the area filled with various tables, chairs and couches.

"This is the main room. It's a lot busier in the evenings, especially if we have a party going."

"Great, you made it back. You must be Cindy, I'm Scout, president of the Charon MC. It's good to finally meet the woman who's had Nitro in knots for so long."

I felt my face heat and had no clue how to respond to his comment.

"Shut the fuck up, prez. Quit embarrassing my old lady."

My breath caught as Scout's eyebrow went up and he lifted a hand to stroke his beard.

"That didn't take long."

Nitro's arm snaked around my waist and pulled me tight against his front. "Yeah, well, I ain't letting her run off on me again. I want my patch on her back and my ring on her finger."

I turned my face so I could glare at him. "Were you planning on actually asking me if that's what I want?"

He winked down at me and kissed the top of my head. "I already know it's what you want. But if you're good, I might ask before I slip a ring on your finger. Or you know, you might just wake up one day with a ring on."

I shook my head and chuckled. He was so ridiculous. And I was very glad that he was all mine.

Chapter 10

Nitro

I had no doubt it wouldn't be long before Cindy was wearing my patch and my ring. I refused to accept anything less. Maybe I should talk to Natalie about learning how to tie her up so she couldn't get away from me ever again. That had me grinning. The more I thought about the BDSM thing, the more I liked it. I mean, it's not like I haven't been doing some of it forever, I just didn't realize what it was called. Or that there was so much more than the little bit I'd tried. I couldn't wait to go to the training session at Titanium on Sunday.

"When you get a minute, I got something for you in my office. Not sure if you want it now or later."

I cocked my head to the side trying to work out what he was talking about. He wrapped his hands around each side of his cut and gave it a small tug and I grinned in understanding.

"I was hoping your habit of reading the future would hold true for me. Thanks, prez." I paused to look around at who was still hanging around in ear shot. "Keg! Can you take Cin down to the kitchen and make her a coffee?" I turned Cin around and kissed her fast and hard. "I'll be five minutes max, okay, babe?"

She shrugged and I could tell that brain of hers was working overtime.

"I promise, there's nothing for you to worry about, and you'll be safe here in the clubhouse."

The fact Keg had been guarding her so much over the past week should help her feel at ease. But she really didn't look sure.

"Nah, don't worry about it, brother. I'll have one of the boys take it up to your room while you show your girl around. Welcome to the Charons, Cindy. You're family now, and we take care of what's ours. You ever need anything, just let me know."

With that, Scout ducked back down the hallway and Keg followed after him.

"Right, okay, well, I guess we'll continue the tour." I pointed at Scout and Keg's retreating forms. "The offices are down there." Leading her down another hallway, toward the rear of the building we passed a closed door that I hadn't wanted to mention, but I should have known better than to try to slip it past Cin. Of course she was going to be curious about everything in this place. Most people were, initially.

"What's in there?"

"That's nothing you need to worry about. It's the whore room. The club whores aren't allowed to wander around the clubhouse til after ten pm. If there's kids around and they're caught outside that room, they get booted."

She winced but didn't say anything. I hurried her further down the hall and into the kitchen.

"It's pretty quiet at the moment—this is probably the emptiest you'll see this place. Normally old ladies only come here in the evenings or during the day on the weekends when we have a family barbecue. Not really much reason for the ladies to be here outside of those times. Whenever you're here, you're welcome to eat and drink whatever you want. There's always at least a few of the prospects and brothers living here, so the kitchen is stocked with all sorts of food and beverages."

"Prospects?"

I winced a little, kicking myself for not having already explained all this shit to her.

"Ah yeah, there's levels within the club. If a man wants to become a Charon, he starts off being a hang-around, which is literally just that. They come to the parties and maybe the charity runs or poker runs we do, then if the club likes them, they move up to being a prospect. Keg and Jazz are prospects. They have a cut, but they don't have all the patches on the back yet."

With a nod she added, "I noticed that."

"Generally speaking, you spend about a year as a prospect. Sometimes they get in faster, sometimes slower, it's not a specific amount of days or anything like that. Both Keg and Jazz are actually about due to patch in as full members.

"Once they've done their time as a prospect, it gets taken to church for a vote, and assuming everyone is cool with it, they get patched in. Then they can call themselves a brother, and wear the three patches on the back of their cut, or vest. Once they're a full, patched in brother, they can get voted in as one of the officers. There's the president, vice president, secretary, treasurer, road captain and sergeant-at-arms."

"Okay, I can figure out most of those jobs, but what does a sergeant-at-arms do?"

"I'm basically responsible for the safety and security of the club—"

"Whoa. Wait, *you're* the sergeant-at-arms?"

I grinned at her. "Yeah, baby. Scout's the president, Bulldog is the VP, Keys is the secretary, Arrow the treasurer, and I'm the road captain and SAA."

She looked impressed, and I had to admit, it did wonders for my ego and pride.

"So you're basically the cop of the Charons?"

And just like that, my glow was dimmed. "I wouldn't say it like that. Ever. Please don't tell people I'm a cop. MCs don't like cops as a general rule, probably got something to do with the fact we don't always play within the law."

She came up to my front and wrapped her arms around me. "You don't need to defend your distrust of cops to me, Nitro. Trust me, after all these years of them ignoring me when I've needed their help, I'm not exactly a huge fan of law enforcement myself."

I held her a little tighter at her words. I couldn't believe the cops had been so dismissive of her case.

"We do have friends down here at the local station that we call on when we need to. I might reach out, or get Scout, to ask if they know why your reports were discarded so quickly. Something smells about that situation, and it might help pinpoint who is after you."

"I had wondered over the years if my stalker was a cop."

I nodded and pulled my phone out to text Keys. "I'll tell Keys to look at any police who shifted from Bridgewater to Houston around the time you left."

With a strained smile and a sigh, she pushed away from me.

"Show me the rest of this place?"

Following her lead, I let the subject drop for now. I took her hand and led her out into the backyard.

"Here's where we spend a lot of evenings. We get the bonfire going and sit back and relax. We're planning on building a cubby and some play equipment over there now that we've got more kids coming along."

It felt like a damn baby boom in the club lately. Had to be something in the water. I tightened my arm around her waist. I'd taken her bareback and she could be pregnant right this moment. That fact had me grinning like a fool. Creating a life together would be the ultimate bond between us.

"What's that look for?"

Her tone was more than a little suspicious.

"Nothing at all, babe. Just feeling good."

Feeling in the mood for a little fun and games, I grabbed her and tossed her over my shoulder, ignoring her shriek, and gave her ass a slap as I carried her inside, then upstairs to the bedrooms. Knowing the door would be unlocked from Keg coming up earlier, I pushed my way in and kicked the door shut behind me, being careful not to let it hit Cin. After giving her ass another tap, I set her on her feet. Then, before she could open her mouth, I wrapped my palm around the back of her neck and slammed my mouth over hers.

Whenever I was anywhere near Cin, my cock was on alert, but right now it was fucking hard enough to pound nails. With my free hand, I pulled down the zipper on her jacket and started to shove it over her shoulders. She followed my lead and shrugged out of it, letting it fall to the floor. Breaking the kiss, I made fast work of stripping her shirt over her head and unclasping her bra.

"Fuck, you're so damn beautiful."

Cupping her breasts in my palms, I alternated between kneading them and tweaking her hard little nipples until she was squirming for me.

"You'll be my old lady, won't you, Cin?"

She groaned and wrapped her fingers around each of my forearms, but when she didn't try to push me away, I kept tormenting her body.

"Tell me yes, babe. Say you'll be mine."

Arching her back so her breasts pushed further into my palms she moaned before licking her lips, and with hooded eyes, looked up at me.

"I've always been yours, Johnny."

With a broad grin stretching my lips, I gave her nipples one last tweak before I reached past her to grab her cut off the chair there. I slipped it up one arm and with a gasp, Cin froze for half a second before she moved to help me slide it on her fully. Once it was sitting as it should, I took a step back, and wanted to take a fucking photo.

"Fuck me, babe. That's the hottest thing I've ever seen."

Biker boots, tight as fuck jeans and my property patch were the only things covering her sexy body. My cock was throbbing with want now and I made fast work of stripping out of my own clothes as she stood there running her hands over her new cut. Since she was so focused on her cut, and not me, she didn't realize I'd stripped until I stepped up close to her, making her jump.

"Need to be inside you more than I need to breathe, babe."

As fast as I could, I had her jeans unbuttoned and shoved down over her hips, her lacy panties going the same way. Leaning her over the bed, I ran my fingers over her slit, testing to see if she was as desperate for me as I was for her.

"Fuck, you're so wet. You want this as much as I do, don't you?"

"Uh huh."

Pulling my hand away, I lined up my cock and slammed home, groaning when her channel clenched hard around me. With her jeans holding her legs together, she was tighter and I knew I wasn't going to be able to last long, especially when I looked up to see the back of her cut. "Property of" was written on the top rocker, while "Nitro" was written on the bottom one. And it had my cock jerking, on the verge of coming already, seeing her wearing my property patch.

"Love you, Cindy."

I paused for a moment to lean down and nip at her shoulder before I kissed the same spot. Wrapping her braid around my hand, I tilted her head and took her mouth, dancing my tongue with hers, letting my body cool off just a touch. Once I felt more in control, and didn't think I was going to blow any second, I released her mouth, and ran a palm over her hip and up her torso. When it was resting between her breasts, I lifted her upper body up so she was kneeling in front of me. She leaned back and wrapped her arms around my head, digging her fingers into my hair. The position had her tits thrust out and the cut fell to the sides, framing them. Lifting my hands, I shoved the leather further out of the way and pinched at her tight, little tips. In response, her body clenched down on mine and I couldn't hold back a second longer. Shifting my hands to firmly grip her hips, she fell forward onto the bed, putting her hands out to catch herself, as I started a hard fast pace, thrusting deep inside her. She mumbled between her gasps but I didn't catch any of the words. My mind was spinning as my focus zeroed in on her—on us—on where our bodies were joined.

Cindy

Every thrust he made into me had my nipples rubbing against the rough inside of the leather of my cut. He'd worked them into tight little peaks earlier and they were so unbelievably sensitive now every slide of the leather over them sent sparks of arousal through my system. I was going to explode. I tried to hold it off, to prolong the torturous pleasure.

While Nitro had stripped himself naked, he'd been too impatient to strip me completely. The moment he'd shoved down my pants and spun me around, I'd gotten slick for him. His desperation for me was the most potent aphrodisiac I'd ever experienced. His tight grip on my hips didn't allow me to move much from the waist down, but my hands were free. As I spiraled closer to the edge, I tightened my hold on the bedding as my body burned hotter.

"Please, Johnny…"

"What, babe? What do you need?"

I couldn't form words anymore, all I could do was whimper as I sat right on the edge. With a low chuckle that sounded more than a touch evil, he moved one hand around until he could reach my clit. A moment later, he flicked it and my orgasm shot off like a fourth of July firework. I screamed out his name as I bucked and came. My vision went white as a strong climax rolled through my body.

When my mind came back online, I was naked and nestled against an equally naked Nitro on the bed, his large hands stroking my back and arms as he nuzzled his face against my hair. My hands were pressed against his pecs, and I flexed my fingers for a moment, before I pushed myself away from him a little so I could look up into his face. He was looking down at me with a lazy grin and a spark in his gaze and I realized in that moment how much I loved him. And this wasn't like the love I'd had for him as a teenager, this was a stronger, more potent kind of love.

It was a love that scared the shit out of me and froze my tongue when I knew I should tell him how I felt. He's told me, and it must be hurting him that I haven't returned the words so far, but I just couldn't seem to get those three little words to pass my lips yet.

"Kiss me?"

"Always."

He leaned down and I closed my eyes as his lips brushed against mine, once, twice, then his tongue licked over my lower lip. Opening for him, I moved my tongue so it was dancing with his. Warmth curled through my body until I wriggled against him, feeling his cock harden against my stomach.

With a groan, he pulled back. "As much as I'd love to stay here all day and keep making love to you, I've got to get over to the bar and sort out that paperwork and shit."

Since his face was out of my reach, I leaned in and nipped at his chest, before I gave it a lick. He growled, and wrapping my braid around his hand, he pulled my face away from his skin.

"Feeling frisky today, babe?"

He bit at my jawline then kissed me hard and fast once more before releasing me and rolling over. He held out a hand to me once he was standing.

"C'mon, up you get."

Taking his hand, I allowed him to help me stand up. Once on my feet, he handed me my panties.

"No shower?"

He gave me a slightly feral grin. "I'm feeling a little possessive right now and like the idea of knowing you're wearing me on your skin."

I rolled my eyes, but slipped my panties on. He'd obviously cleaned me up while I'd still been out of it, so it was just a little sweat. I got a lot sweatier at a derby game, so didn't have an issue letting Nitro have this one.

Within ten minutes we were both fully dressed and heading back downstairs. As we walked through the main room, I pressed my nose to my shoulder and inhaled against the leather. *Hmmm, always did love that smell.* Back out by the bikes, Nitro took my jacket and packed it away in one of the saddle bags while I attempted to get the helmet strap done up. It was harder than it looked without being able to see what I was doing, especially since it was a completely different buckle from my derby helmet, but I got it sorted by the time Nitro was ready to go.

He'd rolled his bike out of the line-up so I had more space to hop on. With a hand on his shoulder, I put my foot on the peg and lifting myself up, settled on the warm seat behind him. The sun had heated up the leather of the seat and it was warm enough I could feel the heat through my jeans. The moment I had my palms up under the front of his shirt, he revved the engine and took off, with two other bikes following behind us.

A few minutes later he pulled up in front of a café. I couldn't see anything that looked like a bar near it and I frowned as I swung my leg over the back of the bike and dismounted as the two bikes with us pulled up beside us.

"This isn't the bar."

He wrapped an arm around my waist and pulled me in for a quick kiss.

"Nope, it's not the bar. Figured we'd make a pit stop to grab something to eat before we head over to Styxx. This is Marie's Cafe. Marie is Scout's old lady, and there's always a few of the Charons in here. Especially now she's pregnant."

That had me pausing in my steps. Scout had looked to be old enough to be a grandparent, not a father. How old was Marie?

"Don't look like that. Their story isn't so different from ours, but Marie didn't run off. It was Scout who emotionally abandoned Marie, even though neither of them ever actually left town. Thankfully, they finally got their shit together and now they're happily married with an adopted daughter and another child on the way. You'll like Marie."

Mac slapped Nitro on the shoulder as he walked past us.

"Yep, only took them, what? Twenty years to stop torturing themselves. My old lady, Zara, works here as well. And my little lady should be in here too."

Nitro guided me through the door before I could respond to Mac and I found myself in a cozy looking cafe.

"Dada dada!"

"Hey there, baby girl, I'm coming for you."

There was a playpen in the corner that held a young girl bouncing on her butt, reaching out toward Mac as he walked over to her. The second he was close enough, he scooped her up and she squealed in delight.

"Already a daddy's girl that one. Hi! I'm Zara, Mac's old lady and that one's momma. You must be Cindy."

I glared over at Nitro for a moment, without much heat. "Does everyone in Bridgewater know my name?"

He looked a little sheepish, but it was Zara who laughed and answered my question.

"Can nearly guarantee everyone in the club does. You'll discover, Cindy, nothing spreads quite like a rumor in an MC."

Mac came over to us with his daughter bouncing in his arms and jabbering away in baby talk. He leaned over and gave Zara a kiss.

"Hey, babe, she been behaving herself?"

Zara laughed again. "As much as she ever does. Little spitfire, that's what you are, aren't you, Cleo?"

She grinned over at her mother like she was an angel, but you could see it in her eyes she had a spark in her that I was sure meant she tested her parents constantly.

Zara clapped her hands. "Right, well, ya'll find a table and I'll bring over a round of coffee. Did you want anything else?"

"A couple slices of whatever pie Marie has going would be great. Gotta introduce Cin to Marie's Cafe properly."

With a shake of her head and another chuckle, Zara headed off to the counter as Nitro guided me over to the table nearest the playpen. Mac came with us and the closer we got, the louder Cleo got.

"Whoa, baby girl. I'm not putting you down."

It wasn't until he sat with her sitting on his lap that she settled down. Clearly she really didn't want to go back into the playpen if her daddy was around.

"She knows what she wants, huh?"

Mac grimaced a little. "You could say that. This one is gonna keep us on our toes, that's for sure. Only six months old and already trying to rule the world."

A pang of envy hit me as I watched Mac lean over and grab a toy zebra out of the pen and hand it to his daughter. What kind of father would Nitro be? Would he be attentive like Mac was? There was something about watching the big, tough biker being so sweet with his daughter that had me wishing for things I wasn't sure would ever be possible. We'd had unprotected sex again today, but even if I did manage to become pregnant, I had no idea what my stalker would do about it. Would he finally come after me? Try to hurt the baby? Or would he come for Nitro?

My stomach rolled and when Zara slid a large slice of apple pie in front of me, I winced, not sure I could stomach even a mouthful of it, even though it looked and smelled delicious. The moment she'd set my coffee down, I dumped some sugar and cream in, gave it a quick stir then lifted it to take a mouthful. The brew helped settle my stomach but the nasty feeling of what my stalker could do to hurt Nitro or me remained in the back of my mind.

Chapter 11

Nitro

Something about little Cleo had set off Cindy in a big way. I saw her shut down and pull away as she watched Mac playing with his daughter. Did she realize I'd taken her again earlier without a condom? We really needed to have another conversation about that. She'd passed it off as no big deal after the first time, but I was starting to think that wasn't truly how she felt. I let her be while Zara delivered the pie and coffee, and frowned when she jumped on the dark brew like she needed it more than air. Mac caught my gaze and raised an eyebrow, I shrugged in response. I had no clue what was up.

"Well, Miss Cleo, let's go see if we can find something for you to eat that won't make as much mess as a piece of pie will. Maybe find Gramma so she can come meet Cindy."

I appreciated him giving me a moment, especially when Cindy didn't seem to notice them getting up and walking away. I reached out and stroked my knuckles down her cheek.

"Cin? What's up? Talk to me."

She blinked a few times as she took another mouthful of coffee, then after carefully placing the cup down she turned to face me, and the devastation in her gaze hit me like a punch to the gut.

"What if you've gotten me pregnant? What will my damn stalker do when he finds out? Will that be what sets him off and makes him come after me to hurt me? Or you? Will he do something like make you wreck on your bike?" She shook her head as tears filled her eyes. "I can't lose—"

Her voice broke and she covered her mouth with her hand. I scooted my chair back and pulled her into my lap so I could cuddle her in against me.

"Even if you're already pregnant, we're going to deal with this fucker before you start showing enough for him to know what's going on. I'll keep you safe, Cindy. And I'll keep myself safe. I'm not a teenager anymore, I'm a fully trained SEAL, baby. We don't go down so easy. And you? You're a fucking roller derby girl. I've seen how rough that shit gets. You won't go down without a fight, either."

I hated that she was so skittish, but I couldn't blame her. I'd wondered myself how this bastard would react to finding out she was pregnant, if she was in fact pregnant. He was clearly unstable, and my coming back into her life had rattled him. Burning down Retro Funk was a very impulsive thing to do. I was quite sure it wasn't a well-thought-out plan, but rather a knee-jerk reaction to finding out I'm still hanging around. Hopefully that meant he made mistakes and we could catch the fucker.

"How about we start using protection again until we get your stalker dealt with? I want to take away the things that are stressing you out, not add to them."

Swiping her fingers over her eyes, she took a deep breath before she twisted around so she could pull me down to kiss me.

"You're too good to be true, you know that?"

I had no response to that. I could see love in her gaze, and hear it in her tone, feel it in her kiss and touch, but she hadn't said the words yet. I wasn't sure what I needed to do to make her feel secure enough with me that she could admit her feelings, but I was determined to figure it out. I needed to hear her say the words she used to give me so freely.

With a small sniffle, she slipped off my lap and back onto her chair.

"So, this pie is supposed to be the best in town, right?"

"Damn straight. Marie has a gift when it comes to baking pies. No matter the flavor, they're all good."

Using a fork, she carved off a small piece and when she wrapped her lips around the tines, I had to rearrange myself to relieve the pressure. Her groan of enjoyment didn't help my situation any.

"Oh, this is good."

Her next bite wasn't a dainty little piece like the first one. Nope, once she discovered she liked it, she plowed through the piece of pie in no time at all. With a chuckle,

I moved my plate closer to her so she could have at my piece too. The moment she saw it, she froze and her cheeks grew redder before she gently placed her fork down and wiped her mouth.

"Babe, don't be embarrassed. I like seeing you enjoy yourself."

"And I love to see people enjoy my food."

I smiled up at Marie and stood for a minute to give her a hug. "Hey, Marie, I'd like you to meet my old lady, Cindy. Cindy, Marie. Scout's keeper."

She scoffed and playfully smacked my arm. "In my dreams I keep that man under control. Hi, Cindy, it's lovely to meet you and I'm glad you're enjoying my apple pie."

Before she could say another word, Cleo started up as Mac came back over.

"Dada dada!"

Marie's face lit up as she turned to face the child. "Well, hello, my sweet girl. Did your daddy come in to say hi?"

Mac laughed when the little girl planted a wet kiss on his cheek after he sat back down with her. The chime over the door tinkled a moment before Silk came blasting through, nearly taking out Zara, who happened to be walking past at the time.

"Sorry. Where is she? What's she like?"

Deciding to cut Silk off before she said anything else, I called out.

"Silk! Getcha ass over here and introduce yourself, before you embarrass yourself."

The woman didn't even look sorry at being busted talking about Cin. She hitched little Raven up higher on her hip and rushed over. After she settled her eight-month-old son into the playpen, she turned her attention on us.

"Hi! I'm Silk, Eagle's old lady. Not sure if you've met him yet. Love your ink."

Silk had always been full on, but since hooking up with Eagle and having a baby, she was even more in-your-face. I wasn't sure how Cindy would take her, but I shouldn't have worried. Anyone with as much ink as my girl had, would be an instant hit with Silk.

"Thanks." Cindy pulled her sleeve up. "I've got ink on my arms, neck, legs and back. If I had more money, I'd have more, but damn, tatts add up fast."

Silk was holding Cin's forearm and turning it so she could see the large tattoo of a pin-up chick on roller skates that covered her bicep.

"This is some really good work. Where'd you get it done?"

"Ah, that one was by this guy over in Austin. He's a huge roller derby fan so I got a good deal after we won this big tournament there a few years back."

Both women were grinning and I relaxed back into my seat after sliding the plate of pie back in front of me. I shouldn't have worried about how the old ladies would treat Cindy. You couldn't not love her. And I should have known that just like the rest of the club, the women would have my back and Cindy's.

"Well, you need any more ink, you come see me down at Silky Ink. First one's on the house."

Zara groaned as she came back over to the table and wrapped an arm around Mac's shoulders.

"Cindy, just don't let her choose the tattoo for you."

Silk glared at Zara. "I will get that playboy bunny tatted on you one day, mark my words."

Zara turned on Mac. "Have I mentioned lately how much I hate that everyone knows you call me bunny?"

Mac smirked at his woman and I shoveled more pie in my mouth as I attempted to contain my laughter.

"Well, bunny, maybe if you hadn't run off on me so many damn times, I would have picked something else."

"Rara!"

With a shake of her head, Zara picked up Cleo and put her in the pen with Raven to play. Or rather, to snatch the toy off Raven that he was playing with. Damn, that girl was possessive.

Once the coffee and pie were all gone, I looked at the clock and winced.

"Well, as much fun as this is. I do actually have to get some work done before we head back to Houston tonight. Cin? You want to stay here with the girls or come see Styxx with me?"

She looked so relaxed and happy, I hated to pull her away, but I wasn't making shit up. I had bookwork to get done before I could take off with her again.

"I'd love to see where you work. And you know, I have worked in a bar for a damn long time. I'm sure I can help you."

A surge of happiness flowed through me at her words—that she wanted to help at the bar. Hopefully, that meant she'd be open to moving here soon, to moving her life to Bridgewater. I was sure we'd be making regular trips up to Houston for the rest of our lives, and that didn't bother me one bit. But I wanted our home here and our kids to grow up here with the other Charon kids.

Cindy

I don't know what I was really expecting the other old ladies to be like, but these ladies weren't it. Even though I realized the term old lady didn't mean the women were old, for some reason that's where my brain went. But even Marie, who was a little older than the others and me, still had plenty of life and sass in her. I really liked all the women I met while we were at Marie's Cafe, and the babies were completely adorable too. Once I got over my little panic attack about my own biological clock, I'd enjoyed watching the two of them. Poor little Raven looked to be a little older than Cleo, but quite clearly, Cleo was the boss. That kid was going to drive her folks insane by the time she hit her teen years, I was sure.

"Oh, before you go, give me your phone."

I wasn't sure exactly what Silk wanted my phone for, but Nitro didn't seem upset by her demand, and it wasn't like I had anything on there that I wanted to hide from the world, so I reached for my pocket.

"Ah, why?"

She grabbed my phone the moment I held it out toward her.

"So I can put all our phone numbers in, of course. Next time you're in town, we'll have to be more organized and sort out a girls' night. Us old ladies stick together. We're family…"

She trailed off as she typed rapidly into my phone, and I glanced at Nitro, who was looking way too pleased with himself for some reason.

"What are you planning that you have that look on your face?"

Instantly his expression blanked, making me even more suspicious.

"Not planning a thing, babe. C'mon, let's get moving."

I didn't believe him for a moment, but got caught up saying goodbye to the girls before I could quiz him about it further. Then I was the one grinning because I got to go for another ride on Nitro's bike.

"You really love it, don't you?"

I smirked over at him. "It's fast and has wheels. Of course I love it!"

That had him shaking his head with a chuckle. "C'mon, Evel Knievel, on you get."

I gave his shoulder a light smack before I climbed on behind him.

"Cheeky man."

Then we were off again. It was only a short ride over to the bar, and no one followed us this time so it was only the rumble of Nitro's Harley I could hear. I was already used to the throaty sound the machine made, and couldn't wait for our ride back to Houston, when I could have enough time to really enjoy the wind in my face and the freedom of being on the motorcycle.

He pulled up at the rear of the building and my feet had barely hit the ground before Nitro was on me, shoving me up against the wall and taking my mouth with his in a rough kiss that was all desperation. With a moan, I opened up to let his tongue dance with mine as I wrapped my arms around his neck.

"Fuck, babe. I want you again, but I really need to get this shit sorted out. You working tonight?"

I tried to catch his lips with mine again, wanting more of his kisses, but he shifted and buried his face against my throat before he lifted up and nipped at my ear.

"Answer me, Cin."

"Yeah, working tonight. But don't have to go to practice. Kiss me."

"If I keep kissing you, I'll end up fucking you and then either you'll miss work tonight, or I won't get the payroll and ordering sorted out."

With a pout, I lowered my arms. As much as I wanted to have more of Nitro, I wasn't so selfish that I'd risk people getting paid late, or leaving Natalie in the lurch when I didn't show up.

"Fine. Well, let's get it done as fast as we can then, maybe we'll be able to fit in some sexy fun times after we ride back to Houston."

He shook his head with a grin. "You really like riding that much?"

"I truly do. Thinking I might need my own bike." I paused when he growled at me. "What? Are old ladies not allowed or something?"

He scrubbed a palm over his face while he unlocked the door and punched in the security code. After flipping a bunch of switches, he started walking down a dark, timber-paneled hallway before he finally answered me.

"Old ladies can ride. Silk has her own bike, but if the club's going somewhere officially, she's on the back of Eagle's bike. My issue is I fucking love how you feel pressed up against my back as we ride. Need you on my bike with me for that. And I know you well enough to know that the moment you get your own ride, I'll be hard pressed to get you off it and on mine ever again."

I did my best not to laugh. He was most likely right.

"Wow, this place is nice. Very dark and biker-like."

He froze as he was about to open a door off the side of the hallway, to turn and glare at me.

"Very dark and biker-like? What the fuck does that mean, exactly?"

I waved a hand around, enjoying the hell out of teasing him.

"All this. Everything in here is dark and dim. Is the main bar area the same?"

"People can see what they're drinking."

His voice was gruff and sounded hurt as he shoved the door open. Then he let loose a string of curses that I was pretty sure had nothing to do with my opinion about all the dark and gloom. I moved around him into the small room and whistled at the desk.

"You weren't kidding about the paperwork."

"Fuckers didn't do a damn thing all week. I wasn't expecting this much of a mess. Fuck it all, this is going to take me for-fucking-ever to get through."

Moving to stand in front of him, I ran my palms up his chest under his cut in an attempt to try to calm him down a bit.

"I'm here to help, Nitro. What do you want me to do? I can go check out the bar, make sure it's all stocked and the storeroom is in order. Do you have a ledger of what should be in stock?"

His arms tightened around me, holding me to him for a few moments before, with a sigh, he released me and moved toward the mess on the desk.

"Yeah, there's a ledger in here somewhere. Doubt it'll be any use. Fuck." He scrubbed his palms over his face. "Right, okay. If you could go check on the state of the bar and the storeroom, then come let me know the damage. Hopefully by then I've found the ledger for you."

Nitro was looking so pathetically sad, I rushed over and kissed him loudly on the lips.

"Cheer up, babe. We'll have this sorted out in no time. You'll see."

His expression didn't indicate he believed me, but I'd show him. With a little bounce to my step, I left the office and continued down the short hallway until I found myself in a large room, which was like I suspected, more of the dark and gloomy. But then it was literally a biker bar, so I guess this is what the men wanted it to look like. My mind started coming up with ideas for improvements but I pushed them aside for the moment. Today was all about getting what was already here sorted out. Later I could chat with Nitro about my ideas.

I made a quick lap around the area and was impressed with how clean everything looked. Clearly they had cleaners come in to go over the place. The bar itself had been kept clean and well-stocked by the look of it, with only the odd bottle missing on the racks. So at least the boys had kept the front of house up to par in Nitro's absence. I wondered what the storeroom was going to look like.

Heading back down the hallway, I paused for a moment to glance in on Nitro. He was fully engrossed in sorting all the papers into piles. His face was pulled into a nasty glare and I really didn't want to be whoever had been left in charge in his absence. I doubted the conversation was going to end well for them.

Back near the rear entrance was another door on the opposite side from the office. Pushing it open, I ran my fingers up the inside of the door frame, flipping the switch when I found it.

"Ah, fuck."

This was almost as bad as the office. Boxes had been shifted around and I couldn't see any kind of obvious order. There had to be one. No way would Nitro have this room anything less than sorted perfectly. As I slipped off my cut and hung it on a hook on the wall, I looked around for a place to start. The pile of empty boxes seemed logical, so I headed over toward them and started tearing them down and making them into a pile.

There were so many, I couldn't take them all out in one trip, so I propped the rear door open so I had a clear path to the dumpster that was out in the parking lot. First trip went off without a hitch. On my second run out, I'd just released my armful of cardboard into the bin when my head was suddenly jerked back. Some fucker had grabbed my braid and yanked on it, hard. With a shriek, I pin-wheeled my arms out to try to catch my balance. Before I could attempt to twist free from the grip on my hair, a jab of pain flared in the side of my neck.

"What the f—"

My words were cut off when suddenly, a big arm wrapped around my middle, tight enough I had to focus to breathe. Or maybe that was due to whatever he'd drugged me with. I was roughly dragged backward and the realization I was being kidnapped shot through my brain, slamming adrenaline through my bloodstream. I tried to scream but before I could get a sound out, the hand from my hair slapped over my mouth.

"Shut the fuck up, bitch. You made me do this. It's all your fault."

It was my stalker, it had to be. I tried to fight my way free, but my arms and legs wouldn't work right. I couldn't do a damn thing but watch the open doorway into Styxx and safety get more distant as my stalker dragged me away.

Chapter 12

Nitro

Heads were gonna fucking roll for this mess. How hard was it to put shit in piles? Or fucking call me if they got stuck? But no, someone, or most likely several someones, had just started dropping stuff on the desk in here and shutting the door. I hated to think of what Cindy had found in the storeroom. The cleaning crew that came in twice a week would have the main bar area looking neat, I hoped. But I bet that back storeroom was a bigger mess than in here.

"Yo! Nitro? What's this door open for? Where's your girl?"

Arrow's voice had me instantly on full alert. A quick glance at the clock had me cursing and rushing to get out from behind the desk. I hadn't realized how much time had passed. Bolting down the hallway, I shoved Arrow aside to get into the store room.

"Cindy!"

The room was empty. I could see where she'd started cleaning up empty boxes and knew she must have started taking them out to the trash. In seconds I was out the back door and beside the dumpster. The parking lot was empty aside from my and Arrow's bikes.

"Motherfucker!"

My voice echoed around the lot as my blood rushed through my system. Her stalker had her. He'd fucking snatched her right out from under my fucking nose. With a roar, I turned and threw a punch at the bin. The front caved in under the pressure and the sting across my knuckles helped me focus. I needed Keys, needed to see the feed from the camera back here. I went to grab my phone when I heard Arrow on his.

"Need you, man. Cindy's been snatched from Styxx. Yeah, from the back lot. Not so great. Yeah, gotcha. Be there soon."

He hung up and came over to grab my shoulders so I was forced to look him in the eye.

"Listen up, brother. We will get her back. I'll ride to the ends of the earth with you until we do, but right now I need you to find your calm. I'm gonna run in and lock up, then we're going over to the clubhouse. Keys is doing his thing with the cameras and her phone."

Of course, her phone. I'd turned on the GPS tracker Keys put on all the girls' phones the first chance I'd gotten. So long as that was on her, we could track her.

"My keys are on the desk."

"I'll grab them. You wait here, no running off on your own—got me?"

After a nod, he released me and jogged into Styxx. My gut twisted as reality crashed through me. A sick, twisted fuck who had been fixated on her for nearly two decades had her. My girl was in danger and I didn't know where she was. Rolling my shoulders and neck, I paced in front of the bin as I waited for Arrow, but stopped when something caught my eye. Crouching down, I glanced under the edge of the dumpster and saw the end of the plastic plunger of a syringe. Standing back up, I ran for the door and bolted into the storeroom. Grabbing a zip-lock bag and a glove, I ran back out. Arrow called out to me but I ignored him for the moment. He'd work out what I was up to soon enough.

Back out at the dumpster, I put the glove on and after opening the bag, leaned down and grabbed the syringe. Carefully, I pulled it out from under the bin and quickly got it sealed in the bag and my glove off and in the trash.

"You think that was used on your girl?"

I strode over to my bike and put the needle into my saddle bag. "Why else would it be here? My girl is out there, drugged and alone. Where are my fucking keys?"

We don't tolerate hard drugs in Bridgewater, never have. And if someone in town did decide to shoot up, no one would be fucking stupid enough to do it behind the club's bar. No, I was certain that needle had been used on my girl. It was the only reason why she hadn't fought and screamed out for me. I should have heard her.

"Fuck!"

Arrow handed me my keys but didn't release them straight away. "You level enough to ride? Because you wreck, that ain't gonna help your girl, you hear me?"

"I'm level enough to ride. I'm just fucking furious I didn't hear anything. Didn't fucking save her."

Releasing my keys, Arrow slapped me on the shoulder. "You will. We'll get her back. The whole club will help you do this, brother."

I'd always loved being a Charon, but whenever shit hit the fan, I was reminded exactly how good it was to be a part of this awesome family.

"Thanks, brother. Let's ride out."

We got to the clubhouse and the place was pumping. Arrow's call to Keys had set things in motion and every member who was able was here to help me get my woman back. After parking in the front of the line-up, I was up the steps and through the door in seconds. Figuring Keys would be still sorting through video feeds, I ignored everyone milling around in the main room and ran for the offices, not stopping until I was standing in front of the man.

"He's got her, doesn't he? That fucking bastard of a stalker has her. Keys, talk to me, man. What happened?"

He looked up briefly and the grim look in his gaze didn't ease the tightness around my chest.

"Still can't work out who the fuck he is. Bastard wore a baseball cap. It kept his face hidden. Cindy was taking out torn down boxes to the trash. When she was dropping the second load in, he came up behind her and grabbed her, drugged her and dragged her away. Looks like she tried to fight, but he caught her by surprise, got the needle in before she could do much."

I tossed the bag on the desk. "Found that under the dumpster. Used a glove, so I didn't touch it."

Keys' eyes flared for a moment. "Hopefully that'll mean we can figure out what the fuck he gave her so we can counteract it when we find her."

"I'm just waiting on her GPS to load up. Fingers crossed that'll be pay dirt for us and we can ride out. I've got a trace going on the plate, too."

I paced the room as we waited, my mind running over all the shit Cindy could be going through right now.

"Fuck!"

I never should have left her alone at Styxx, or let her go outside. Fuck, why didn't she come and tell me what she was doing? I never would have let her take that shit outside on her own. Why didn't I fucking take Keg or Mac or someone else with me to Styxx? I scrubbed my palms over my face.

"We'll get her back, brother, and we'll make whoever took her fucking pay."

Scout had come in while I'd been pacing. I didn't respond to his statement, I couldn't. I wanted to believe we'd get her back, but this fucker had been obsessing over her for nearly twenty fucking years. I had no idea what he would do to her before I could get to her.

"I followed a few cameras and he's headed south, out of town. And he ain't being careful. Stupid fucker's gonna get pulled over by the cops if we're lucky." He paused for a minute and hit a few keys. "The plate was a bust. It's a stolen van."

"He's being reckless. I doubt he's planned any of this. Like the fire, he's doing stupid shit without thinking it through."

Which could either mean he'd fuck up and we'd catch him fast and get Cindy back, or he'd fuck up and it would cost me my girl's life. Scout moved to block my path, looking like he'd asked me something and was waiting on an answer.

"Sorry, prez, what'd you say?"

"You can't think of anyone this might be? Anyone from your high school days who you've seen around lately?"

I closed my eyes and thought back over the last couple weeks, on everyone I'd seen around Houston. No one stood out. I shook my head. As I opened my eyes, my gaze caught on the clock behind Scout and for a moment, the breath froze in my lungs at how long had passed already. She'd been gone for hours. Fucking hours.

"Can't think of anyone. Keys? This fucker's had her for way too long already. Tell me you have her location, brother."

"Stupid fucker hasn't tossed her phone. He's got her on a boat. She's currently in the middle of Galveston Bay heading toward the outlet."

"I'll call Joaquin and see if they can get someone out on a boat to shadow him for us."

Joaquin was the new president of the Iron Hammers MC, who were based down in Galveston. I was sure someone on their crew would have a boat, or at least access to one. Scout wrapped a palm around my shoulder, getting my full attention.

"And Nitro, I know this is personal, but you need to be the club's SAA and road captain right now, not Cindy's old man. Get your ass out there and organize the club to get this done. Focus on that."

I took a deep breath and gave my president a nod before I headed out of the office. Scout's words were just what I needed to hear, to help me focus on what was important right now. I needed to get my club organized and ready to roll out. Later, once I got my hands on her stalker, I could be Cindy's old man. The moment I entered the main room, everyone went silent.

"I need anyone who can drive a boat or who is good in the water. Chances are high we're gonna get wet on this one."

Cindy

With a dull, throbbing pain, my brain came back on line. For a moment, I thought I must be home in bed with the flu or something. But then I tried to move, but couldn't and memories flooded back to me. Licking my dry lips, I took a couple breaths and tried to listen for anything that might be near me. It felt as though I was swaying, even though I'd been restrained on a chair. I couldn't hear anything other than the soft drone of an engine, so lifting my head, I blinked clear my vision to take in my surroundings. A quick glance confirmed I was alone, then I focused on the window and frowned. What the fuck? I was on a boat? I could see land, but there was a lot of water between here and there. Could I swim that far? In the open ocean. After being drugged. I shook my head, quickly deciding that would be a last resort. I'd never been that strong of a swimmer, not like Nitro had been. Tears pricked my eyes as I wished he were here with me. Why hadn't I told him I loved him? I knew my stalker would catch up to me at some point, why had I held off telling him how I felt about him?

Taking a deep breath, I shut down all my emotions, not having time for them at the moment The longer I took, the further away the boat would be from home. I wriggled my hands and grinned when I heard the clank of metal. My thumbs were double jointed and I could maneuver the joint so my thumb lay flat against my palm, allowing me to slip out of cuffs if they weren't put on too tight. After I'd mentioned it at Titanium one Sunday, the Doms had tested me out a few times. Apparently it was a neat party trick. I was grateful I'd mucked around doing it now, because getting out of these cuffs was my first priority right now.

After testing the tightness of the cuffs, and discovering they were fairly loose, I rotated my thumb joint until it slipped in against my palm, then with some wriggling and a few tugs, my hand slipped free. With my hands now in front of me, I made fast work of getting my other hand free, rubbing at the scrapes it had left up the lower parts of my thumbs and below my little fingers.

The cuffs looked like cheap metal ones you bought at a costume store. The Doms at Titanium would be mortified that someone had actually used them as real cuffs. The fact they were certainly nothing a cop would ever use had me wondering once more about who this guy was. I'd often suspected he was something to do with law enforcement, but this basically threw that theory out. I shook my head. It didn't matter who he was. He was a nut-job, whoever he was, and I now had a pair of cuffs I could use on him if I got the chance. I quickly pushed the moveable arms of the cuffs all the way through so they were reset and ready for use, then sat them on my lap. After I got my legs free, I'd put them into my back jeans pocket so I could grab them easily later if I needed them.

It only took me a few minutes to work the knots on the rope holding my legs to the chair loose, then I was free. Well, I was free from the chair, anyway. Carefully, I made my way to the doorway. Silently opening the door, I poked my head out to see I was at the end of an empty hallway that had a few closed doors down each side and a living area at the other end. The driver, or captain, or whatever the fuck you called the person driving a boat, must be on the level above me. This was one big fucking boat. A lot bigger than any of the fishing boats I'd been on as a kid, that's for sure. Considering how far out in the Gulf we must be by now, I guess that made sense. A smaller boat wouldn't have been able to make it out here. Whoever had grabbed me, hadn't let me see his face so I still had no fucking clue who it was and I couldn't think of anyone I knew, or had known, who would own a fancy boat like this one. I paused as another thought hit me. He might not be alone. I had some hope of catching one person by surprise and cuffing him to something. Hopefully. But if it was more than one, I had no chance at all.

I paced back up and down the hallway for a few minutes, trying to decide what the fuck I should do. When the boat suddenly slowed down, I stumbled into the kitchenette, where I found my phone sitting on the bench. I snatched it up and shoved it into my pocket without looking at the screen, because if he was stopping the boat, it was probably because he wanted to check on me. The land I could see out the windows was still a long way off, so he definitely wasn't docking. By the direction the boat was traveling and the side of the boat the land was on, I figured he must be heading toward Mexico. Had he planned this all out, or was he winging it? Either way, I really, *really* didn't want to end up in Mexico with this nut-job.

When the boat slowed further, the sound of the motor quieting, my heart rate tripled as I tried to find somewhere fast I would fit to hide. A hatch by my feet caught my eye and I pulled it open. A blast of engine noise filled the air, and without another thought, I slipped down the ladder, pulling the hatch closed after me.

"Fuck, fuck, fuck."

I cursed as my ears started ringing instantly from the noise down here. Pulling my phone out, I was surprised when the screen lit straight up. He hadn't even turned my phone off? I hoped Nitro had been telling the truth when he'd told me about Keys being able to track it if anything did happen to me. I hit the flashlight app and shone the light around the space to reveal all sorts of machinery I'd never seen before in my life. The engines were easy to spot. There were two of the big bastards and they were both running. Hopefully he'd think the noise would put me off coming down here and not look for me here.

I moved further into the space. Making it to the back of the room, I noticed other hatches that, at a guess, would take me to the rear deck of the boat. Maybe if I waited for him to come down in the kitchen, I could rush out one of these before he reached me. But then what? We'd start a coyote and roadrunner race around the boat until one of us got tired? I shook my head. That was a shit idea.

Suddenly the engines stopped altogether and the silence was deafening. The sound of heavy footfalls above me had me panicking that he might come look down here. After a quick glance around, I noticed a small area behind what looked like a tank of some sort. Maybe the drinking water? I shook my head. I didn't give a fuck what it was, so long as I'd fit in the space behind it and it would have me out of sight of the kitchen entrance. If he came down through one of the deck hatches I was fucked, but I had to go with the options I had available. Flipping off my flashlight, I curled up as small as I could and prayed if he came down and looked around, he wouldn't be able to see me in the dark.

Then I waited.

The longer I waited, the tighter my chest got and the harder it was to breathe. And the more I started kicking my own ass. What the fuck was I thinking? How was hiding going to help? It sure as fuck wasn't going to stop him from taking me to Mexico. I wasn't a scared teenager anymore, so I needed to stop acting like one. I was a strong fucking woman who could handle this shit.

Standing up, I moved out of hiding, and now that my eyes had adjusted some to the darkness, looked around at what I had to work with. I figured the easiest way to prevent him from taking me anywhere would be to disable the engines somehow. If we were stuck out in the ocean, eventually the Coast Guard would come to check out the problem, wouldn't they? Or Nitro would find me. He had to be tracking my phone by now, surely. I could maybe find a way to sneak into where the radios were and call for help. Although, that was two levels up from where I currently was, so at this point, that wasn't my most realistic option. I did decide that basically, anything was better than simply waiting here like a sitting duck for him to find me.

Turning my flashlight back on, I glanced around until I spotted a small toolbox. Slowly, and quietly I went over to it and opened the lid, taking out an adjustable wrench and screwdriver. The hammer would make too much noise, so I left that behind. Then I turned to one of the now silent engines. I was no mechanic and really had no fucking clue how to best stop the thing from being able to start again, but I figured if I undid all the hoses and pulled off all the wires I could, it would cause enough problems to stop it from working. However, I didn't really want to get covered in gas, so I figured I'd start with the wires. Putting down the wrench, and tucking my phone into my bra in such a way that the flashlight was shining past my top and out in front of me, so I had two free hands, I began to methodically undo screws and pull out wires. Praying all the while I didn't electrocute myself. Once that was done, I turned my attention to the hoses. Figuring the smaller tubes would be for fuel, I focused in on the larger ones that looked like they'd be safe to take off. Grabbing the one closest to me, I set about unscrewing the hose clamps. I managed to get it loose, and then gave it a massive tug to pull it completely off. Which worked, and sprayed green water—at a guess, coolant—everywhere. I jumped back to avoid the spray and froze when a hand wrapped around my hair and held me in place. I threw my elbow back but another palm wrapped around it, holding it up behind my back.

"What the fuck do you think you're doing, Cindy?"

That voice! I knew that voice, but from where? He hitched my arm a little higher when I didn't answer him and I snapped out of my shock. It didn't matter who the fuck he was, I needed to fight. I'd put the wrench down unfortunately, but I still had the screwdriver. I switched my grip on it and using all my force, slammed it back into his thigh.

"You fucking bitch!"

He shoved me away from him, and I managed to retain my hold on the now bloody screwdriver. Not that it helped me as his shove landed me hard against one of the engines. I'd ended up going head first toward the metal but thankfully I'd managed to get my arms up before my head hit. Pain shot down my forearms at the impact, but thanks to so many years of roller derby, I was used to rolling with the pain after taking a knock. He threw a fist into my stomach, but I'd seen it coming and had clenched my abdominal muscles, preventing me from being completely winded by the shot. However, the punch did dislodge my phone, sending it to the ground where it landed face up so the flashlight filled the entire space with a dull glow.

Ignoring the pain, I made the most of the light and reached for where I'd left the wrench. I'd dropped the damn screwdriver when I'd hit the engine and I had no fucking idea where it was now. The moment my fingers wrapped around the handle of the wrench, I tightened my grip and swung that bitch with all my strength. Knowing I had to hit hard and fast if I was going to win here, I didn't stop to plan out my shot, and the wrench was already in motion before I looked at my target. He was looking down at his thigh, as he held the injured leg with both hands. Obviously, he'd wrongly assumed his gut punch would have left me on the ground writhing. Fucking moron. Nothing kept a derby girl down for long. The tool hit his shoulder with a loud crack and he went down to his knees with a howl of pain.

I grabbed the cuffs out of my pocket and quickly slapped one on the wrist on his uninjured arm and the other on a metal pipe that was screwed into the side of the boat. Before he realized what was going on, I had that fucking thing as tight as I could get it around both his wrist and the pipe and was out of his reach. Snatching up my phone, as I stepped further away from him.

My lungs burned as my breath rushed in and out. I had more adrenaline pumping through my system than I'd ever had before. My hands started to shake, but I didn't drop that wrench or my phone. Scanning the light around the walls, I found a switch. Flipping it up, the area filled with light.

"What the fuck do you think you're doing, little girl? I'm gonna make you pay for this, mark my words. I'll do more than burn down your precious shop."

That had the breath catching in my throat but I refused to rise to his taunt. He couldn't do a damn thing to me anymore.

I slipped my phone back into my pocket as he smirked at me for a moment before he went back to wincing. The shoulder I'd hit was slumped down, like he could somehow get away from the pain if he cowered enough, and the blood coming out of his thigh had soaked into the material of his jeans, and was forming an ever-widening stain.

"Yeah, you made me mad when you went out with that fucker Harris again last night. You knew you weren't allowed. I lost my temper and when I drove past that little shop you love so much, I got this idea. It was fun, you know? The shatter of the glass, the whoosh of the flames. The smells and the heat. Thing of beauty, it was. You should have seen it. I stayed to watch for you, to see your reaction but that bitch of an aunt of yours didn't call you when she was supposed to, so I fucking missed seeing you. She was supposed to call you and cut your night short, you were supposed to fucking learn! I thought I made myself clear a long time ago about you not seeing that bastard."

I shook my head in shock. I mean, clearly the guy had proved long ago he was a nut-case, but he was completely certifiable! And I still couldn't fucking place him and it was starting to get annoying.

"Who are you and why the fuck have you made my life hell for the past two decades? What did I ever do to you?"

Before he could answer, a noise behind me had me spinning around with the wrench up, ready for action, and my heart, which was just starting to slow, kicked up a notch again. Would the day never fucking end? And

how many people did I have to fucking knock out before
I could go the fuck home?

Chapter 13

Nitro

It was a glorious thing to be able to call on a team of men you trusted fully to have your back, no matter what. It took less than ten minutes after I walked into the main room of the clubhouse and stated what I needed for a team of men to be ready to roll out. Scout had gotten hold of Joaquin and he'd been more than happy to offer us whatever help we needed. The moment Scout had called, the Iron Hammers president had sent his man, Blade, out in his boat to keep track of Cin from a distance. When we'd finally arrived at the dock, Joaquin had been there waiting for us with another boat, all fueled up and ready to go.

Now we were racing across the Gulf as fast as his boat could take us to get to my girl. Blade had radioed through that the yacht had stopped and dropped anchor, which meant two things. We'd catch up to them faster, which suited me just fine, but it also meant if he wasn't captaining the boat, he was doing other things. That had me growling. The very thought of Cin being hurt burned me down to my soul.

"Relax, brother. We'll get there and get your girl. She's stayed one step ahead of this fucker for nearly twenty years. She's proven she can be resourceful. I'm sure she's found somewhere to hide herself away until help can arrive."

I turned to Taz. "Do you hear the words coming out of your mouth? Has Flick taught you nothing about strong women? You should see how rough that derby shit gets. No way is my Cin cowering in a corner, waiting for me to save her. Nope, she'll be fighting like a hellcat to get free, and that's what scares me. That he'll kill her before we can make it to her because she won't know when to lay low and wait it out."

Before Taz could respond, we caught up with Blade's boat and I shifted into warrior mode.

"He left the bridge about fifteen minutes ago, hasn't come back. I think you'll be fine to approach and board without any trouble."

"Yeah, if he's below deck with her, we need to fucking hurry. This baby is nearly silent at low speed so they shouldn't hear us. Right men, get ready to jump ship."

I gave Joaquin a nod and gripped the side of the boat as he took us closer to an anchored, fancy-ass yacht. The closer we got, the harder I tried to see in through the windows but I couldn't see any movement. Joaquin proved he was really damn good with a boat and got us right up alongside the other vessel.

"Head down to the engine room first."

I looked back at the other club's president, curious to how he could possibly know that. "Don't bother thinking about how I know, just go deal with it."

With a nod, I jumped, landing lightly on the rear deck of the other boat. I was about to grab the hatch in front of me when I heard Cin's voice come from inside the cabin. Following the sound, I found an open hatch in the kitchen. Mac and Taz had both followed me inside and I gave them a signal to let them know I was going down.

"Yeah, you made me mad when you went out with that fucker Harris again last night. You knew you weren't allowed. I lost my temper and when I drove past that little shop you love so much, I got this idea. It was fun, you know? The shatter of the glass, the whoosh of the flames. The smells and the heat. Thing of beauty, it was. You should have seen it. I stayed to watch for you, to see your reaction, but that bitch of an aunt of yours didn't call you when she was supposed to, so I fucking missed seeing you. She was supposed to call you and cut your night short, you were supposed to fucking learn! I thought I made myself clear a long time ago about you not seeing that bastard."

The voice floated up and I froze to the spot. It was a voice I hadn't heard in forever. Not since before I went to BUD/S training. Fuck it all, I knew who her stalker was and I had a feeling it was all my fault. Guilt ate at me as I slowly climbed down the ladder to the engine room while Cin responded.

"Who are you and why the fuck have you made my life hell for the past two decades? What did I ever do to you?"

Seeing she had him restrained, I relaxed a little and purposefully made my next step heavy enough to make some noise. With a jerk, she spun around with a wrench lifted, ready to strike. Made me proud of her, really. Ready for anything, that was my girl.

"Relax, Cin. It's just me and a few others from my club. Mac and Taz are up on deck, and a few more are in the boats we came in. It's all over now, baby. You're safe."

Her shoulders slumped for a moment then re-tensed. "It's not fucking over until he tells me why, and who the hell he is."

"You don't recognize him? I'd know that whiney bitch, fucking voice anywhere. Looks like you've had better days, Coach Smith."

"Fuck off, Harris."

Stepping forward, I took the wrench from my girl's hand and tossed it aside before I wrapped her in an embrace. Fuck, it felt good to have her safe in my arms again. She wrapped her arms around my waist and rested her cheek against my chest.

"So, have you worked out why he did all this shit? Because I only had him for gym class, I didn't do the swim team or any other sport that I spent much time in his presence."

"Not sure, babe. Guessing he was originally aiming at hurting me. Feel like telling your story, Winston? While you still can?"

He sneered at me and tugged at the cuff that had him attached to the pipework. Fuck, I really was proud of my girl.

"Holy shit, brother! You weren't joking about your girl being tough. She done him up good."

Cin tensed and glanced at where I'd tossed the wrench.

"Relax, babe. That's just Taz. You'll like his old lady, Flick. She wasn't at Marie's today, but you'll meet her real soon, I'm sure. Flick put Taz on his ass in front of half the club in Stxx when they first started dating. Funniest thing I've ever seen. Former Marine put on his ass by a slip of a woman."

"She was an FBI agent, fully trained. It wasn't like I got taken down by a kid or anything." He sighed. "I really wish everyone would forget about it. Listen, it's getting pretty cramped down here. Can we take this upstairs?"

"Yeah, just give us five, then we'll be up."

Taz vanished up through the hatch and it was just the three of us again.

"So, Winston, you gonna share your secrets or not? Honestly, I really don't give a fuck but apparently Cin wants to know."

"You'll never get away with—"

"Shut the fuck up with your threats. You've spent enough time in Bridgewater to know what the Charon MC does to bastards like yourself. So, spill your story or not, I really don't care, but hurry up and make the decision. I'm impatient to get my girl home."

The light down here was dim but it was enough that I saw when fear filled his gaze. Yeah, now he was getting it.

"Fuck you."

Or maybe he wasn't.

I turned away from him, guiding Cindy up the ladder where Taz was waiting to help her up before I followed her, not giving the bastard who'd tormented her for years another look.

"Do you think we'll ever know why?"

"Now we know who it is, we can search his house and see if we can find any clues. But I've got some ideas as to what his reasons might be. We can discuss that later. Right now, I want to get you off this fucking boat and on our way home."

"What'll happen to him?"

We were now out on the rear deck of the yacht. I pulled her to me and wrapped a hand around the back of her neck before tilting her face up with my other hand.

"You don't need to ever worry about him ever again. He'll never bother you. That's all you need to know, okay?"

"Okay."

Her voice was a whisper and I lowered my head, giving her a hard, fast kiss before releasing her to move over to the side of the boat, where I helped her climb up until Arrow could grab her and lift her onto our boat.

"Give me one minute, then I'll be over there and we can get going."

I didn't give Cin time to argue before I turned to head back below deck to where Taz was now guarding Winston.

"He doesn't seem like much. I mean, your girl nearly killed him with a screwdriver and a wrench. Why the fuck didn't she just do that years ago?"

"Because he's a sneaky fucker who she couldn't identify. Didn't help the cops didn't believe her. You see, this little shit liked to claim accidents. Tell me, Winston, did you actually scare that feral hog out onto the road in front of her parents' car, or did you just claim it for your own?"

"I aint telling you shit, Harris."

"Yeah, figured you just claimed that first one. Let me guess, you saw an opportunity to hurt me through her because I had a Navy recruiter sniffing around me?"

The way he clenched his jaw told me all I needed to know.

"Then I guess you grew fixated on her and forgot all about me. Cin is a pretty special girl, but she was always mine, never yours. Even after seeing your face, she didn't even know who you were. Wanna know how she reacted when she saw me for the first time in over eighteen years? No? I guarantee you she knew exactly who I was the second she saw me." I shook my head as he sat there sneering at me but refusing to say a word. "You're pathetic. You never would have made it in the Navy, much less as a SEAL. You aren't man enough to make it through BUDs."

I pulled a knife from the clip on my belt and stepped closer.

"As much as I'd love to leave you to drown when we sink your piece of shit boat, I want to be one-hundred percent certain you're fucking dead more. So, lucky you, you get a quick end, one you in no way deserve."

With a deep slash across his throat, the deed was done.

"I need to get back to Cin and check her over for injuries. I didn't see any blood on her earlier, but I want to be sure. Can you frisk him and check the boat for anything of interest before Blade and his crew take this thing wherever the hell they're going to take it to sink it?"

"Consider it done, brother. Mac and I'll head back with Blade and his crew if you guys need to leave before we get done."

"We'll wait for you. I feel like a shit for not doing it myself, but I want her in my sights and she doesn't need to spend any more time on this fucking vessel."

Taz slapped me on the back as he moved to climb up. "That's what you have brothers for, mate. We've got you."

After wiping my blade clean on the dead man's jeans, I put it away and followed Taz up and out of the engine room and headed toward the boat where my woman was waiting for me.

Cindy

The bunch of men on the boat were a mix of guys I'd met earlier today and a few new faces. I was very grateful I'd spent some time with the club because if I hadn't known any of these men, I would have freaked the fuck out when Nitro didn't follow me over. I'd turned to call out to him after I was safely on the other boat, but he'd already moved back inside.

He was going back down to see Winston, I knew it. My gut rolled as tremors shook my body. Lurching for the side of the boat, I managed to throw up over the side and not in the boat before I slumped down against the deck. It was like all my energy had drained away as I'd tossed my guts.

"Whoa, sugar. It's okay. You're safe now."

Arrow scooped me up and carried me back toward the cabin of the boat. I wanted Nitro. I twisted around to try and find him but I couldn't see him on either boat.

"You don't need to see anything that's going on over there, sugar. Here—" He paused as he set me on a soft couch. "Let me grab you a bottle of water. Nitro will be here in your face, making demands before you know it."

I knew he was trying to cheer me up, but I wasn't feeling it. I pulled my knees up against my chest and curled up against the back of the couch and watched the big man move around the interior of the boat. This one was smaller than the other one, with only one level for everything. I tried to keep my mind busy by taking in all the features of the boat but it didn't work for long. Tremors continued to wrack my body as I processed what I'd done. I'd stabbed a man. And there'd been a lot of blood. I pressed a hand over my mouth as I gagged again. Had I hit an artery and killed him? Had I taken a man's life today?

"Whoa, don't mess up the boat, babe!"

A different man, one I didn't know, put a bucket in front of me, but my stomach was empty, I had nothing left to bring up. Arrow went to hand me the bottle but when I reached out a shaking hand, he pulled it back and unscrewed the top before placing the cold plastic against my palm.

"Small sips at first. Don't want to upset your stomach any more than it already is."

I couldn't help but groan as the cold liquid slipped down my throat. Closing my eyes, I took deep breaths between my small sips, trying to get my body to stop shaking. With a gasp, I jerked when a blanket was wrapped around me. I looked up to see it was Arrow once more taking care of me.

"Thank you."

"You're welcome, ma'am. Everyone on this boat is either a Charon or an Iron Hammer, and we're all here to keep you protected. I promise, you're safe now and Nitro will be here soon. Do you need anything else?"

I tried to smile at him as I tucked the blanket in closer around me. "Just Nitro. Thanks again for the water and blanket."

He nodded with a grim smile before he turned and headed to the rear deck of the boat. I closed my eyes again and focused on my breathing, while my thoughts went right back to what I'd been wondering before. About whether I'd killed a man today.

"Ah, fuck."

Before I could lift my head, which was suddenly feeling extremely heavy, Nitro had me in his lap, nestled in against his warm body. Forcing my eyes to open, I looked up at his face.

"Did I kill him? I didn't mean to, I just wanted to get away."

"Shh, Cin. You did what you had to. You don't have to worry about him ever again."

Panic rose up inside me. What was he saying exactly?

"I need to know, Johnny. I need to know if I killed a man, or if he's still alive."

He stared into my eyes for a minute before he seemed to understand he wasn't going to be able to brush off my questions, not about this.

"You didn't kill him. But he is dead. I'm not giving you anything more than that, and you can't tell anyone that he's dead. He needs to just vanish without a trace. Do you understand?"

I nodded my head as I thought over what this meant. A wash of relief filled me. Not only was I not a murderer, I no longer had a stalker either. A small smile tugged at my lips. "So it's really over? I'm free?"

He grinned and leaned down to press a kiss against my temple. "Yeah, babe. It's all over. You never have to look over your shoulder for him again." His expression grew serious again. "Did he hurt you at all? Any wounds that need checking?"

I shook my head. "I got my arms up in time to save my head when he shoved me against the engine. I'll probably have some bruising to my forearms—oh, and probably some bruising on my stomach where he gut-punched me too. But it's nothing. I've copped worse from crashing out at a derby game."

Another shudder ran through me and I huddled in closer to his body, needing to be as near to him as I could get. He pulled the bottle from my hands and passed it off somewhere then took my hand between his and turned it over.

"You were cuffed?"

"I woke up on a chair, hands cuffed behind my back and my legs tied with rope."

His fingers gently rubbed over the scrapes up the side of my hand.

"How'd you get the cuffs off you and onto him? And how did you get down into the engine room to begin with?"

The thick Aussie accent of Nitro's friend Taz came from behind me.

"I can slip out of cuffs if they're not put on super tight. Once I had them off, I saw they were the cheap crappy kind that you can push the arms through to reset. So I reset them in case I got the chance to use them. Once I got free I was pacing the hallway trying to think of something I could do. When he slowed the boat, I stumbled into the kitchen and found my phone along with the hatch to below deck. Figuring hiding somewhere other than where he left me was a good start, I went down there. When I saw the engines, I thought if I could stop them from working, the Coast Guard would eventually come looking. It wasn't the best plan, but it was all I could think of at the time. So I grabbed the screwdriver and wrench and set about pulling off wires and hoses."

I was sure Taz wanted more details, but I was trying really hard not to think about what happened in that engine room.

"Wait, you can slip free of cuffs? How the fuck do you do that?"

Grateful for something not injury related to focus on, I wriggled my hand out from Nitro's grip.

"Double jointed thumbs, see."

I swiveled the joint in and out a couple times before I pulled my hand back under the warmth of the blanket. Nitro's palm followed and wrapped around mine again.

"Holy shit, that's some party trick."

The engine below us came to life, and I jumped before relaxing again. Suddenly everything seemed so hazy and I couldn't quite hold onto a thought.

"Johnny? Why am I so sleepy?"

What was wrong with me? Had I hit my head earlier? Or was whatever drug Winston had given me still in my system? His arms tightened around me as he pressed another kiss to the top of my head. "You've had a big day and are worn out, baby. Go on and close your eyes, I've got you. When we get back to Bridgewater, we'll have a doctor look you over, make sure nothing's wrong. I'm guessing you're just crashing after the adrenaline rush, but I want to make sure."

"Uh huh."

Pressing my nose against his shirt, I inhaled and caught his scent. He'd taken off his leather vest, but the smell lingered in the fabric of his t-shirt. It was my new favorite scent, and I let myself drift off to sleep. Knowing with one-hundred percent certainty that Nitro would keep me safe while I rested.

Chapter 14

Nitro

Joaquin took things slower on our return trip, which meant Cin stayed fast asleep in my lap, even when Arrow, Taz and Mac came to sit around us.

"She threw up after you left her. I think she might be in shock."

I nodded to Arrow. "Yeah, that and adrenaline crash. I'm sure she'll be fine after she gets some rest. Thanks for taking care of her. Things got rough down there. She fought hard."

"You're not kidding. That girl would give my Flick a run for her money. Stabbed a screwdriver into the fucker's thigh, and smashed his shoulder with a wrench before she cuffed him to a pipe. Girl's got grit."

"Sounds like the perfect kind of woman for an old lady."

I gave Arrow a feral grin. "Damn straight she is. She's fucking perfect. Always has been." I looked over to Taz. "Find much on the boat?"

"A few things. Looked like he was planning on settling down in Mexico. We've got his address in Houston and some other stuff. I'll give it all to Keys to sort through when we get back. Was he really your coach back in school? That's fucked up."

"Yeah, I only had him for a coach in my senior year. I was always good in the water so I was on the swim team. I'll see what Keys finds, but I'm pretty sure he got jealous when a Navy recruiter came sniffing around me. Then he noticed my girl and got fixated."

I took a deep breath and looked down at her face, lax in sleep. I couldn't believe all the shit that happened to her all stemmed from the fact I'd fucking loved her in high school. Taz nailed it. It was totally fucked up.

"What do you want to do about the story behind today? We can't wait to figure it out, she was supposed to work tonight wasn't she?"

I squeezed my eyes shut. "Fuck. I didn't message Natalie to let her know she wouldn't be in."

What time was it? It was getting dark out so it meant it was late, late enough she should be at work by now.

"Get Cindy to call her once we dock, but we'll need our story straight by then. What do you want to do?"

We were definitely going to have to figure out a story to tell everyone about what happened out here. The crew in at Titanium would definitely be worried with her not turning up without warning. And the fact she'd now told all her teammates about her stalker. Fuck. Her bruises to her arms would need an explanation. Not to mention

Winston's disappearance. This wouldn't be the first time the Charons had recreated reality, and I doubted it would be the last.

"We need to keep it close to the truth. This shit is going to get messy no matter how we play it. How about we say what happened, except instead of what went down on the boat, we have Cin getting out the cuffs then jumping off the boat and swimming for it. We were close by and picked her up. While we attended to her, he took off and we didn't bother giving chase."

Arrow laughed. "Donald will know that's a load of shit. The Charons not give chase?"

I gave him a small shrug. "Don't give a shit if they believe it or not, the facts back us up. We have the video footage of him snatching her, plus the syringe. Half of Bridgewater would have seen the pack of us riding south when we came to get her. And now we'll head back with her intact and no Winston and no boat. By the time they do a search for it, it'll be at the bottom of the Gulf somewhere. If they even bother looking for it. The facts back us up, and they'll never find that body to prove otherwise."

Arrow held his palms up. "You don't need to get defensive with me, brother. Just letting you know what Donald will say."

"Well, considering the fact the police ignored all her reports for the past two decades, trust me when I say if Donald tries to take this up with me further, it ain't gonna end well. I'm sure there's something Cin could sue them for out of all this. So, I think they'll accept our story and move along."

"You think she'll move back to town now?"

Fuck, Arrow was all fifty questions today.

"I'm hoping so. With the shop gone, she doesn't have that tie anymore. And her aunt who ran the store is a stone cold bitch. She's certainly not gonna want to hang around Houston for her sake."

"She has other work right? And she's got a house and her derby shit too."

Arrow was named for the way he shot straight from the hip. Not a bad trait in a man, until he turned it on you.

"Yeah, she does. But she has to move back. I need her. The drive up isn't too long, if I can find her somewhere to skate locally she'll only need to head up to Houston a couple times a week for team practice. And her other work is bartending at this club. Fuck, she loves that place. She's not gonna want to leave anytime soon."

"And you don't want to leave Bridgewater or Styxx. Sounds like you both have some thinking to do if you want this thing you got going to work long term, brother."

"Yeah. I know. I was toying with the idea of getting her a shop in Bridgewater she could set it up like her grandma's place had been. Run it her way, without her aunt breathing down her neck all the damn time."

Maybe we could salvage a few signs or something from Retro Funk, something to put in the new store as a piece of her grandma.

"It's got potential, especially if you get her online as well as a physical store front. She could well end up so busy she won't mind not working at that club of hers. And if you need extra start-up funds, bring it to church. I'm sure the club would be happy to have another business under our belt. She's, what, a little younger than us? She's not gonna want to have to be out all night, every night, forever."

"You know, Zara mentioned the other day that the shop next to Marie's is empty now. That would keep her close to home, and encourage her to befriend the other old ladies. They all seemed to get along well earlier today."

I gave Mac a nod. "Yeah, scary how well they got along so fast. Thanks, brother. I'll check it out."

Taz chuckled darkly. "Brother, just knock her up. Trust me, if you do that, she'll be too tired to care what you do. You can have her moved in with your patch on her back and a ring on her finger before she realizes what you're up to."

Even as I thought about the fact I'd taken her bare again this morning and could have already done just that, I shook my head at the crazy Aussie. "Yeah, because that's how you got Flick to move in. I remember it was her that knocked you on your ass, brother. Not you knocking her up. And I already got my patch on her back. She just took it off to work in the store room at Styxx before all this shit went down."

That got everyone chuckling, except Taz who groaned. Taz needed to accept the fact that he was *never* going to live that one down. It'd been a beautiful moment. Scout set him up by kissing his girl on the cheek when he was standing behind her. Taz grabbed her to pull her away, but Flick hadn't realized who it was and had pulled some fucking martial arts move that had Taz—a trained Marine—flat on his back in seconds. I was grateful the girl chose to do it at Styxx and not the clubhouse. Meant I got to watch.

"Seriously, I know it's going to take some doing, and a little time, but I fully intend to win Cin over and have her in my bed every damn night of the week."

I spent the rest of the trip watching her sleep. She really was beautiful, even covered in dirt, blood and coolant. That had me smirking. She'd done a hell of a job on that engine, pulling off wires then that coolant hose. Bet she got a shock when it burst liquid all over her.

When we finally pulled into the dock, I stroked my knuckles down her cheek.

"Hey, babe, time to wake up."

With a moan, she snuggled in against me but didn't look like she was going to wake up. I didn't bother trying to stir her again, just stood with her in my arms and strode out onto the rear deck. Taking extra care that my footing was stable, I stepped up onto the dock and headed toward where we left our bikes earlier.

"We've got our contact on the Coast Guard looking the other way. We'll let them know what happened, or rather, what we decided happened, later. Get Scout to call me with the fleets when you have them all confirmed."

"Shall do. Thanks for your help, man. Appreciate it."

A haunted look flashed through Joaquin's eyes. The man didn't look like he could be much over thirty, if he was that old. But his eyes, they were not those of a young man. There was definitely something strange going on with the biker, but today wasn't the day I was going to work it out. Shifting Cindy's weight so I could get a hand free, I held out my palm to the other man. He took it in his for a moment before nodding behind me.

"Anytime, brother. Looks like your boys brought down a bus for your woman. I'll leave you to it."

Turning around I was relieved to see that Keys and Donna were both here with our bus. We used that thing way too much lately, but it was a Godsend. A few years ago, we'd tricked out this tank of an SUV as a sort of ambulance. Keys' old lady, Donna, was a nurse and was always happy to step up to get things done. I was beyond grateful I knew who was going to be checking over my girl, that's for sure. Without a moment's hesitation I strode over toward them.

"She been out the whole time?"

"Nah, she was well and truly awake when we found her. She's taken a few hits but seemed physically fine. She crashed on the way back and just now I couldn't wake her. Mind you, I didn't try real hard. I'm hoping she's just sleeping off her shock and adrenaline crash, but I'll feel much better after Donna checks her over."

Donna had opened up the back of the bus while Keys had spoken with me, so I moved over to climb in and put Cin down on the stretcher inside. The moment I released her, she came awake and clung to me.

"It's okay, Cin. We're back on land, you're in the Charon's ambulance. My brother's old lady, Donna, is a nurse. She's going to check you over, okay?"

"You're gonna stay with me, right?"

I leaned down and took her mouth with mine, kissing her deeply because I fucking needed the connection, before pulling away from her to speak. "I need to ride my bike back."

"Nah, you don't. I came down in the cage so I could ride your bike back. You stay in here with your girl."

I turned to look at Scout, who was now standing at the rear of the bus, as my eyes started to sting. Having good brothers was a thing of beauty. It truly was.

"Thanks, brother."

"Charons stick together. We always have each other's back. And don't think I've forgotten what you did for me not so long ago. Now, sit down and let Donna do her thing. We'll see you back at the clubhouse."

I tossed him my keys and with that, he and Keys shut the door and left the three of us in the rear of the vehicle.

"You found something really special with that club, didn't you?"

"Yeah, babe, I sure did."

Sometimes I took it for granted, but not today. Today I thanked God that I'd found the Charon MC and was lucky enough to be able to call myself one of them.

Cindy

No matter how hard I tried to stay awake, I kept dozing off on the drive back to Bridgewater. It was like now I'd allowed my body to sleep once, it was all it wanted to do. With Nitro by my side, at least I didn't have to worry about anything Donna was doing. I knew if she stepped over any line, he'd be on her. But if she was anything like the other women I'd met earlier, which I was pretty sure she would be, I didn't have anything to worry about.

When the van came to a stop and the engine was cut, I forced my eyes open once more just in time to see the rear doors swing open to reveal the man who'd shut us in. Keys, was it? Yeah, definitely Keys. Nitro lifted me up against his chest again before he climbed out. I probably could walk myself but honestly, it felt too good being so close to him I didn't complain like I ordinarily would. Blinking against the bright floodlights illuminating the yard, I watched as several Harleys roared into the parking lot around us. This many had gone down to Galveston to rescue me? Most of them didn't even know who I was!

"They know you're mine, Cindy. That's all they needed to know to drop everything and come help me save you."

Guess I'd said that out loud, I hadn't meant to. Heat rushed to my face.

Nitro's golden Harley came up close to the building before the rider dismounted and pulled his helmet free. Scout, the club president had personally ridden Nitro's bike home. I was completely blown away and speechless.

"She need the hospital, Donna?"

"I don't believe so. Ideally, she would be in overnight to make sure whatever he gave her is out of her system fully, but if she stays here, I can come check on her a couple of times during the night, and she'll be close to the hospital if we do need to take her in."

"Good deal. This will be easier to cover up if we don't have to involve a hospital. Nitro, get her upstairs and cleaned up. I'll get one of the old ladies up there to sit with her when you're ready and we'll sort out what the fuck we're gonna do to explain this shit. Oh, and get her to call whoever she needs to that's gonna be worried about her vanishing act this afternoon." The second he finished speaking, Scout turned to face the others. "Keys, Arrow, Bulldog, I need you three in my office so we can start making plans. Mac, call in Keg and Jazz. They don't need to stay in Houston anymore."

When Scout had turned his focus off us, Nitro had started heading toward the building. He was at the top of the steps when Scout finished. Instead of heading straight inside, he turned back toward everyone. I was wide awake now and the sight of all those bikers in their leathers staring up at us was a sight I don't think I'd ever forget. So many of them, all here because they wanted me safe. It was surreal and mind blowing.

"Thank you, brothers. I won't forget what you all did for me today."

Nitro's voice was rough with emotion and had me turning my gaze up to see his eyes were shining with moisture. Lifting my palm, I cupped his face and he spun on his heel and stepped through the door that was being held open by another of the Charons. He turned his mouth to kiss my palm but stayed silent as he took me inside and upstairs to the same room he'd taken me to earlier today.

After setting me on the edge of the bed, he dropped to his knees in front of me and buried his head in my lap. I shrugged off the blanket and ran my fingers through his hair.

"I'm okay, Johnny. We're gonna be all right."

His body shuddered before he lifted his head and looked straight into my eyes. No tears were tracking down his face, but his eyes were rimmed in red. My heart softened and my whole being melted a little. My big, tough biker was tearing up over me.

"You took at least ten years off my life today, Cin. Fuck. I'm never letting you out of my sight again. I love you, Cin, so fucking much. I need you with me, here in

Bridgewater. I know it won't happen overnight and we have a ton of shit to work through. I know it seems daunting, but we'll get there. We'll do it. Now, who do you need to contact to let them know you're okay? Try to limit the details you give until I confirm with the others the story we're sticking with. I'm guessing we'll go with pretty much what happened—but instead of you cuffing him down in the engine room, you just got out of the cuffs and dove overboard when you saw our boat coming for you. Can you do that?"

I nodded. "Yeah, I might just send off a couple texts. I don't really feel like talking to anyone just yet, anyhow." I pulled the phone out of my pocket.

He snorted out a laugh. "Still can't believe he didn't toss your phone."

That had me chuckling. "He didn't even turn it off. I found it in the kitchen on the counter, still on. He wasn't the brightest kidnapper. I'm kind of surprised he didn't slip up before now really, considering how poorly today went for him."

"From what I learned from him, and you, I think in the past he's claimed shit he didn't do and the things he did do were meticulously planned. Me coming back into your life and keeping you guarded 24/7 threw him for a loop and he panicked, taking a risk to grab you when he saw a chance. Nothing was planned out from what we can tell. Keys will go through everything now and we'll work out exactly what he was up to, but at a guess, he didn't even have anything lined up in Mexico. He'd just watched one too many movies and figured that was far enough away from me to get you to himself."

A tremor ran through me and my gut roiled again. "I figured he was taking us to Mexico. It's why I risked getting caught by damaging the engine like I did. No way did I want to end up down there. Especially if he was unprepared. Fuck, can you imagine what would have happened? We would have gotten caught, he would have been killed and I would have been—" I slapped a hand over my mouth to catch my sob. I didn't even want to finish that sentence.

"No way, Cin. He never would have made it all the way to Mexico. We were on his tail. Blade had already caught up but was hanging back so Winston wouldn't think he was following you, and we weren't far behind him. Thanks to him stopping the boat, we got to you faster, but we were always going to catch him before he reached land."

Wrapping a palm behind my neck, he pulled me forward until he could kiss me. The longer his lips moved against mine, the more my thoughts calmed and before I knew it, I wasn't thinking about anything other than getting Nitro inside me.

With a groan he pulled back, but kept our foreheads touching.

"Need to get you cleaned up first. Send your texts, I'm gonna go get the shower going."

He pressed another quick kiss to my mouth before he rose to his feet. As he strode across the floor, he pulled his shirt over his head and tossed it toward a chair. The sight of his naked, muscular back distracted me for a moment before I remembered what I was supposed to be doing. Waking up my phone, I let out a curse. Renee, Natalie and half the team had blown it up with messages and missed calls. I opened a new group text and told them I was sorry I didn't show up at Titanium for work, that my stalker had snatched me from the street and taken me. I assured them all that I was okay now, that Nitro had rescued me and after I got a good night's sleep, I'd call them to tell them more. After I hit send, I put my phone on the nightstand before I pulled my shirt off, and following Nitro's lead, tossed it on the chair. A quick glance at my forearms showed that I already had bruises coming up from where I smacked into that damn engine.

"Fucker."

I quickly stripped off everything else and made my way over to the bathroom. I was sure Nitro would have come back to carry me in, but I wasn't a damn invalid. I'd just been so bloody tired after everything that I let him do it earlier. But now I was feeling revived, I wanted my man. And I had something I needed to tell him, something I should have told him days ago when I first realized it.

He was adjusting the water when I came in, his sexy muscular back facing me. My gaze caught on his ass and with a sigh, I ran my palms over the tight globes. He really did have the finest ass I'd ever seen.

He chuckled as I pressed myself up against his warm back.

"Hey, babe. Miss me?"

"Yes. You were taking way too long to come get me."

He tugged on my arm until I moved to stand in front of him under the warm spray. It felt so good, I groaned as I tilted my head back and let the water wash over my face and down my body. I went to reach for the washcloth but Nitro growled and took it from my hand.

"Let me, Cin."

Not wanting to waste too much time with the process of getting clean, I washed my hair while Nitro did a thorough job of washing every inch of my flesh. He left my nipples and pussy for last and when he ran the cloth over my nipples in little circles I clenched my legs together against the ribbons of arousal he was creating within my body. Rushing to rinse the last of the shampoo out, I wiped the water from my face and focused on Nitro, on running my hands over his wet skin. Tracing the definition of his pecs and abdominal muscles. His cock was hard and thick and jerked every time I stroked his torso.

Knocking the washcloth from his hands, I pressed myself up against his front, wrapping my arms around his neck.

"I love you, Jonathan Harris. Always have, always will."

He stilled for a moment, then a wide grin spread across his face.

"Been waiting for you to say the words, babe. Fuck, I love you so much, Cindy soon-to-be-Harris."

I gave him a mock glare. "That ain't a proposal, Johnny."

He gave me a smirk. "I know. But it's still the truth." He ran his palms down my body until he had my hips in his grip. "Tell me I can have you, tell me we don't need a condom."

We'd already risked fate a few times, what was once more? And the more I thought about having a baby with Nitro, the more I liked the idea.

Wrapping my hand around his thick erection, I pumped him as I spoke. "Take me, I'm all yours."

With a low growl, he lifted me up and pressed my back against the tiles. I lined up his cock to my core and as I slid down his length, I wrapped my arms and legs around him.

"Feels so damn good, babe. Fuck. I love you, Cin."

I clenched down with my internal muscles and leaned up to nip at his jawline.

"Love you too, Johnny. Now, get moving. I need to feel you inside me."

He barked a laugh, and gave me a mock salute.

"Yes, ma'am." Then he started thrusting in and out of me and my thoughts swirled away as he loved my body so well and long I knew I'd never get my fill of this man. My man. Johnny was all mine, and I was his. Just how it was always meant to be.

Epilogue

Three weeks later
Silky Ink
Cindy

"He still hasn't worked out what you're doing today?"

I glanced up from my thigh to Silk's face. "No clue. I can keep a secret when I want to. Can't wait to see his face."

I'd been working with Silk for the past two weeks on drawing up this design and I fucking loved it. Silk was one exceptionally talented artist, that's for sure. The piece was large, taking up the entirety of the outside of my left thigh. It would be fully visible between my shorts and knee pads when I was at derby games.

"I wish I could be there. He's gonna flip."

She sprayed my skin and wiped before reloading the gun with more ink. I'd already been lying on her table for most of the afternoon, but by the looks of things I didn't have too much longer to go. Maybe another half an hour to an hour.

It was nice to just lay here and relax after the whirlwind my life had been since my kidnapping. I'd now moved out of Renee's place and in with Nitro. The crazy man had leased me the shop he'd told me he would. It was right next door to Marie's Cafe. We were still setting it up for a grand opening in a few weeks. Nitro had even managed to salvage a couple of the signs from Retro Funk that were already installed on the walls of my new place. Since my aunt didn't care for the store name, I was able to take it for mine. I was so happy Retro Funk would live on. I knew I could make Grandma proud.

I still worked two nights a week at Titanium, and Nitro and I went up at least one night a week to play, along with going to the Sunday training sessions. I didn't mind the commute, even when I had to take my car, which wasn't often. Normally Nitro rode with me. Damn, but I loved to ride. I was hoping over the summer I could start learning to ride myself. I was pretty sure Silk would help me out with it. I was sure she wouldn't pout the entire time, like Nitro would.

"Saw you and Nitro deep in discussion with Keys last night. He have news?"

The police had come to see me the morning after my rescue and I'd told them the altered story Nitro had told me to go with. They'd seemed accepting of it and hadn't hung around for long. Although, I did notice Scout pulled one of them into his office for a little while. Not sure what that was about, but guessing it was about Winston's police connections. Nitro had told me that even if the police were not going to look into Winston, the club would. I wasn't sure it was worth the effort, but Nitro said they wouldn't let it go until they worked out if there were others who had been involved over the years. That had gotten my attention and I'd been keeping up with Keys on what he'd discovered as he kept looking into things.

"Um, yeah, he's been looking into Winston, trying to work out how he did what he did and if anyone else was involved. The fact the cops ignored my reports really got to him."

"With good reason. You were an innocent teenager already going through enough without this bastard adding to it. The fact the cops did nothing but brush you off pisses us all off."

I winced as she ran the needle over a nerve. "Yeah, well, Detective Keys has it all worked out. Scout and Keys are meeting with their contact at the station today to discuss it. Not sure why they're bothering, I mean they've never lifted a finger before. I doubt they're going to suddenly care now."

"And unless he's going to pull a zombie, the man ain't coming back to cause more trouble, right?"

I baulked that she knew the truth and she laughed at my reaction.

"Girl, you can tell me the official story all you like, I've been hanging around the Charon MC since I was barely a teen. I know those boys wouldn't have stopped until that fucker was no longer breathing. I don't need to know the details, but I sleep better at night knowing that fucking bastard is sleeping with the fishes on a permanent basis. So, you gonna tell me what Keys figured out? I'm curious, and we have some time to kill while I finish off your artwork."

I chuckled at that. Tattoos this big did take some serious time to get done.

"Well, you know my stalker was my and Nitro's gym teacher in high school, right?"

"I had heard that. He must have been young back then."

"Bridgewater High was his first job out of college. Anyhow, Keys searched his place and found some journals. It turns out he'd been a bit of a troublemaker as a teen. His folks had booted him out of their home and somehow, this cop found him and took pity on him. Took him in. From what Keys could find out, he behaved himself for a little while. Well, I think he might have just been hiding it well, but either way, he knuckled down and this cop helped him get through college and become a coach. He'd wanted to join the Navy and live what he thought would be a high life, but the recruiters that came around to his school dismissed him. When he first met Nitro, he got blindingly jealous by the looks of it. Guess Nitro was everything Winston had wanted to be. When a Navy recruiter came sniffing around Nitro, Winston really got mad. We were together by then and had only recently started sleeping together, so you can guess how we were."

I felt heat spread over my cheeks and cleared my throat when Silk snickered.

"My folks were in a wreck. A feral hog raced out in front of their car one night and my dad swerved to avoid it and hit a tree instead. Winston wrote me a note claiming he'd caused the accident and if I didn't break up with Johnny, er, Nitro, he'd do worse. I told my mom about it and she said that there was no way someone could have caused the accident. So I ignored it, like she told me to. But he did really kill my cat. Poor Whiskers. Fucker ran him over with his car then tossed him on our front lawn for me to find. I took that second note to the cops along with the first one. They blew me off."

"Let me guess, the officer you spoke with just happened to be this cop who had taken Winston in as a kid?"

"That's our guess, but Winston never mentions him by name in the journal. I'm not sure how he would have known it was Winston who'd done it, anyway. I had no idea who my stalker was until after he took me."

"That's fucking bullshit that he knew it was, but did nothing about it."

"That's the thing, I think he did. From what Keys said he read, something happened between the two of them and Winston was royally pissed at him. The man was a fucking nut-job and Keys said the journal reads like that of a madman for half the time, so it's hard to filter out the facts. I think that's the real reason Keys and Scout are going to the station. They want to work out what happened to the cop who took Winston in. Keys thinks Winston may have found some way to take the man out."

"And being Keys, he has to know."

"Yep."

When both our phones lit up with messages, Silk turned the gun off and set it aside.

"Apparently someone wants our attention."

I tapped on the screen to bring up the message.

"It's from Taz. I didn't realize he even had my number."

"Your number's been added to the club group text. OMG! Flick's had their baby!"

Opening the text I read it out loud "I've got myself a daughter. Lola Grace. All's well."

This was baby number three for the Charons in the past year, with Marie's bub due later in the year being number four. I resisted the urge to place my hand over my flat belly. There was no baby in there yet. But I wondered how it would feel to have a little tiny human growing inside me. I glanced up to Silk when I realized she was being way too quiet and was shocked to see she was crying. "Why is that a sad thing?"

"The name." She paused to pull off her gloves and reached for a tissue to wipe her eyes. "Taz's mom and baby sister were murdered when he was a teenager. Their names were Lola and Grace. He has them tattooed on his chest. That they've named their daughter that? Oh, fuck." She paused to mop up more tears.

I was blown away. That was some very powerful meaning behind that little girl's name.

"Told you she'd be here."

At the sound of her husband's voice, Silk flew up from the chair and blocked anyone from seeing my lower half, while spinning to face the front of the shop.

"Dammit, Eagle! He's not supposed to know about this!"

"Darlin', why were you crying?"

She brushed away his question with a wave of her hand. "Taz and Flick's baby. It's nothing."

I was pretty sure who Eagle had brought with him, but wanted to be positive so I twisted around to see if I was right. Yep, I was. And Eagle had brought Raven with him too. I grinned up at Nitro.

"Hey, babe. Hear the news? Taz is a daddy to a little girl."

He grinned over at me as he slowly made his way around the other stations in the shop.

"I did hear that. Also heard you were down here getting inked up without me. What gives?"

Silk was still blocking his view of the work in progress, and it looked like she was going to get her wish and be here for the unveiling after all. Eagle had their son on his hip and he was moving a lot faster than Nitro, so they got to us first. The moment they were in range, Raven all but lunged out of Eagle's arms toward his mom.

"Mama!"

"Hey there, baby boy. You having fun with Daddy?"

Eagle took advantage of Silk being preoccupied to take a look at my leg.

"Nice." He then gave his wife a kiss on the cheek.

Nitro came up to us and leaned against the bench with his arms crossed, looking very relaxed and sexy as hell.

"It was supposed to be a surprise for you, but it's not finished yet. Don't suppose you could turn around and come back in, say, an hour?"

With a smirk he shook his head. "Not a chance, baby. C'mon, shift over, Silk, let me see what masterpiece the two of you have come up with."

"I'm only about twenty minutes off finishing it, so it's nearly done."

Chewing my lip I gave Silk a nod to move to the side to let Nitro see.

I hoped he liked it.

Nitro

The raw ink on Cin's leg wasn't finished, but it was close enough to being done that I could clearly see what it was. My woman was something else. She was getting a large tattoo of a World War II style sailor dancing with a retro woman on skates. I leaned in closer to see the eyes and hair colors matched ours. Silk was an amazing artist and she'd outdone herself with this piece.

"Say something."

I kept my face neutral as I glanced up at her. She was adorably flustered, thinking I wouldn't like it. Crazy girl. Leaning over, I put a hand next to her head to hold my weight as I lowered my face down to hers. Cupping her jaw with my other palm, I took her mouth with mine, kissing her slow and deep until she melted against the table beneath me.

"Babe, I fucking love it. It's perfect."

She gave me a little growl. "That was mean. You scared me."

I gave her another quick kiss on the tip of her nose before standing back up. "That's what you get for not telling me about it before getting it done. Now, Silk, you said twenty minutes? Because we have a baby to go see."

Silk gave her son a kiss on the cheek before she handed him back to Eagle.

"Okay, baby boy, you sit tight with Daddy while Mommy finishes coloring in Aunty Cindy, then we'll go see your newest playmate."

"He's not gonna be happy it's another girl. Cleo bosses him around enough as it is."

I laughed at Eagle. "Brother, Cleo is one of a kind. That girl's gonna boss everyone around no matter who they are. Little Lola won't give Raven any trouble at all. They'll probably end up teaming up to get one over Cleo as they get older."

Silk had snapped on a fresh pair of gloves and the buzz of the tattoo gun filled the air as we all stood there and watched her put the finishing touches onto Cin's newest piece.

"Have you heard from Keys or Scout yet?"

I knew Cin would ask me that question, but I figured with the baby news she'd forgotten about the meeting between Keys, Scout and Donald down at the station was happening today.

"Yeah, Keys caught up with me a little bit ago. Not sure we'll ever know exactly what happened. But with the information we could add from Winston's journals, Donald believes he's identified the officer who took Winston in. It wasn't done officially and he didn't tell others at the station about what he was doing for the boy. So, when the officer was found dead in his home, no one went looking for Winston because no one knew about him. It was labeled a home invasion gone wrong. The house had been ransacked and valuables stolen. It's still unsolved. And Donald believes it was that case that caused yours to be overlooked. The boys were too preoccupied with trying to find who killed one of their own, to take the time to look into what appeared to be a high school prank."

"Holy fucking shit. He murdered the man who took him in? He was a bigger monster than we realized."

She could say that again. I was extremely glad I'd made sure that fucker wasn't breathing anymore.

"Seems like it. Donald knew the officer, who he wouldn't name, and he said that he suspects the man knew it was Winston hassling you, and attempted to deal with it off the record. Donald is quite sure that if he hadn't died, the officer would have done your case due diligence."

"That's just so tragic."

I gave Silk a nod. "That it is."

With that we all fell into silence as Silk finished off the tattoo, then got it doctored up so we could get moving.

"Ready to go?"

"Just let me put my leggings on."

"And I gotta just clean up this stuff. Give us ten."

I followed Eagle and Raven toward the front of the shop where Eagle started pointing out various tattoos to his son while we waited on the women. Finally, they came out, ready to go. There were three other artists working in the shop so we didn't need to lock up or anything.

"Gabs! I'm heading out for a bit. I should be back by my next appointment."

"Easy done. Say congrats for us."

Grabbing Cin's hand in mine, we pushed our way out of the door and into the perfect Texan spring day. The hospital wasn't far so we all headed up the street on foot.

"Did you notice the eye and hair color?"

I gave her hand a squeeze before I released it and wrapped my arm around her shoulder as she wrapped hers around my waist.

"Yeah, babe. I caught the color choices. It's cute. I love it and I can't wait to have a closer look after we get home."

Yep, I intended to have a very close look at every inch of her when we got home later. I fucking loved that she got a tatt that represented us on her. Made me want to do something similar. Maybe I'd have a chat with Silk later and see what she could come up with for me.

"So you two planning to join the Charon baby boom any time soon?"

Silk's question had my heart skipping a beat. I'd love nothing more than to join the baby boom, but it looked like things weren't going to go as smoothly for us as they had for the other couples in the club.

"We're working on it. No news yet, though."

I rubbed my palm up and down Cin's arm as she stayed quiet. Our lives had been a crazy whirlwind these past few weeks, but even despite the chaos, I knew the fact she hadn't fallen pregnant as easily as the other women was weighing on her.

"Ah well, still early days for you two. It's nice to have a little bit of time as a couple before you go throwing a kid into the mix, anyhow. Enjoy it while you can. And if you ever feel the burning desire to not sleep all night or get spit up on, just yell out and we'll loan you scamp here until you get over it."

Silk elbowed Eagle and gave him a glare that would have taken down a lesser man.

"What, babe? You know I love Raven, I'm just fooling around."

I walked a little slower, letting the other couple get ahead of us as we reached the hospital.

"You okay, Cin?"

She smiled up at me. "Yeah, and Eagle's right. We need to get ourselves sorted before adding a baby to the mix but I'd kind of talked myself into it. You know?"

I leaned down and kissed her temple. "I know exactly what you mean. Did the same thing myself, and you'll see, we'll have our own family before you know it. Once the shop is opened and there's less stress in our lives, things will happen as they're meant to. I can feel it in my bones."

I gave her a wink and pulled a stupid face at her and she gave me the chuckle I was looking for.

"And in the meantime we have your brothers' babies to cuddle and spoil."

"Damn straight."

We walked into the waiting room of the hospital and could barely hear ourselves think over the noise. Looked like the entire club had come straight in to meet our newest member. Keeping Cin locked to my side, I glanced around the room at all the happy, smiling faces and realized that this was my whole world right here. My family. Every single person in this room was part of the Charon MC and I was so fucking blessed to be able to claim each and every one of them.

Other Charon MC Books:

Book 1:
Inking Eagle

***The sins of her father will be her undoing… unless a
hero rides to her rescue.***

As the 15th anniversary of the 9/11 attacks nears, Silk
struggles to avoid all reminders of the day she was
orphaned. She's working hard in her tattoo shop, Silky
Ink, and working even harder to keep her eyes and her
hands off her bodyguard, Eagle. She'd love to forget her
sorrows in his strong arms.

But Eagle is a prospect in the Charon MC, and her
uncle is the VP. As a Daughter of the Club, she's off
limits to the former Marine. But not for long. As soon as
he patches in, he intends to claim Silk for his old lady.
He'll wear her ink, and she'll wear his patch.

Too late, they learn that Silk's father had dark secrets,
ones that have lived beyond his grave. When demons

from the past come for Silk, Eagle will need all the skills he learned in the Marines to get his woman back safe, and keep her that way.

Book 2:
Fighting Mac

She's no sleeping beauty, but then he's no prince - just a biker warrior to the rescue.

For the past three years Claire 'Zara' Flynn has been at the mercy of narcolepsy and cataplexy attacks. But after she witnesses a shooting by the ruthless Iron Hammers MC, her problems get a whole lot worse. She's now a marked woman, on the run for her life.

Former Marine Jacob 'Mac' Miller has a good life with the Charon MC. He works in the club gym and teaches self-defense classes - in the hopes of saving other women from the violent death his sister suffered. When the pretty new waitress at a local cafe catches his attention, he wants her in his bed. But there's a problem. She's clearly scared of all bikers. Wanting to help her, he talks her into coming to his class. Mac soon realizes he wants to keep her close in more ways than one. But can he, when his club's worst enemies come after her?

When Zara disappears, Mac and his brothers must go to war to get her back. Because this time, she wakes up in a terrible place... surrounded by other desperate women, and guarded by the Iron Hammers MC. Can her leather-clad prince ride to the rescue in time to save her from hell?

Book 3:
Chasing Taz

He lived his life one conquest at a time. She calculated her every move… until she met him.

Former Marine Donovan 'Taz' Lee might appear to be a carefree Aussie bloke living it up as a member of the Texan motorcycle club, Charon MC, but the truth is so much more complicated. With blood and tears haunting his past and threatening to destroy his future, Taz is completely unprepared for the woman of his dreams, when she comes in and knocks him on his ass. Literally.

Felicity "Flick" Vaughn joined the FBI to get answers behind her brother's dishonorable discharge and abandonment of his family. Knowing Taz was a part of her brother's final mission, she agrees to partner with him to go after a bigger club, The Satan's Cowboys MC.

However, nothing in life is ever simple and Flick is totally unprepared to have genuine feelings for the sexy

Aussie. When secrets are revealed and their worlds are busted wide open, will they be strong enough to still be standing when the dust settles?

Book 4:
Claiming Tiny

Some rules were meant to be broken.

After being raised in foster care, Ryan 'Tiny' Nelson has no plans to settle down. But that idea goes right out the window when Missy shows up at the clubhouse. One taste of the Charon MC's newest club whore and he's hooked.

Love is the last thing on Mercedes 'Missy' Soto's mind when she runs to the Charon MC for protection. But the first time Tiny wraps his arms around her, he captures her heart in the process.

When things start unravelling, Missy panics and runs. Will Tiny find her in time to give her a Christmas to remember, or will he lose her forever once her past catches up with her?

Book 5:
Saving Scout

Nothing worthwhile in life ever comes fast or easy.

Twenty five years after first meeting the Charon MC's president, Scout, Marie is still waiting for him to realize they're meant to be together. But instead, he comes to her asking she hire his ex. Frustrated with his continued rejection, she leaves town for the weekend to clear her head and maybe find a man who'll help her forget her infatuation.

When Scout first met Marie, she was way too young, and he hadn't been looking to settle down. Over the years, he'd never bothered to rethink his stance. When he learns Marie has fled town, he panics and realizes he needs to step up and claim what has always been his. Tracking her down, he approaches her at her hotel and he finally lets the sparks fly.

But before they can ride off into the sunset, trouble brews and Scout is taken by an enemy from their past that neither of them knew had been waiting for them. Can they overcome this latest hurdle to finally find their happily ever after? Or are they doomed to always be apart?

231

www.ingramcontent.com/pod-product-compliance
Lightning Source LLC
Chambersburg PA
CBHW071600110726
47908CB00007B/2184